PUFFIN BOOKS

Dick King-Smith's
Book of Pets

Dick King-Smith served in the Grenadier
Guards during the Second World War,
and afterwards spent twenty years as a
farmer in Gloucestershire, the county of
his birth. Many of his stories are inspired
by his farming experiences. He wrote
a great number of children's books,
including *The Sheep-Pig* (winner of the
Guardian Award and filmed as *Babe*),
Harry's Mad, *The Hodgeheg*, *Martin's
Mice*, *The Invisible Dog*, *The Queen's Nose*
and *The Crowstarver*. At the British Book
Awards in 1991 he was voted Children's
Author of the Year. In 2009 he was made
an OBE for services to children's literature.
Dick King-Smith died in 2011 at the age
of eighty-eight.

Disc   t:

Dick King-Smith's
Book of Pets

PUFFIN

PUFFIN BOOKS

UK | USA | Canada | Ireland | Australia
India | New Zealand | South Africa

Puffin Books is part of the Penguin Random House group of companies
whose addresses can be found at global.penguinrandomhouse.com.

www.penguin.co.uk
www.puffin.co.uk
www.ladybird.co.uk

This collection first published 2017
001

Set in 15/20 pt Palatino
Typeset by Jouve (UK), Milton Keynes
Printed in Great Britain by Clays Ltd, St Ives plc

A CIP catalogue record for this book is available from the British Library

ISBN: 978-0-141-38808-3

All correspondence to:
Puffin Books
Penguin Random House Children's
80 Strand, London WC2R ORL

Contents

Happy
Mouseday

Dick King-Smith

Illustrated by Peter Kavanagh

CHAPTER ONE

After breakfast, Pete sat in his treehouse, thinking. It was Saturday and, for Pete, Saturday was Mouseday.

At breakfast every Saturday, regular as clockwork, he asked his mum and dad if he could have what he most wanted in all the world – a white mouse with pink eyes.

But the answers were always the same.

'No!' his mother said. 'I'm scared of mice.'

'No!' his father said. 'They smell.'

'Why can't you get it into your head, Pete,' one or other or both of them would say, 'that you are not keeping a mouse in this house? Ever!'

So every Saturday, after breakfast, Pete would climb up into his tree-house, thinking . . .

It's no use, they'll never let me, but I'll keep on trying anyway.

5

The treehouse was no beauty. Pete's
father had made it out of odds and ends
of timber and put a tin roof on it. He
had fixed it in a fork of the old apple
tree. It wasn't very big, but it had a door
of sorts, and a kind of window. Inside
there was an old folding garden chair

for sitting on, and a shelf for keeping things on, and the whole treehouse was rainproof.

Most importantly, it was Pete's, and on its side was written in big black letters:

On this particular Mouseday, Pete was thinking about the actual words his mum or dad always used. 'You are not keeping a mouse in this house,' was what they said.

Suddenly he jumped up from his chair. Through the branches, he peered out across the lawn.

'OK, so I can't keep a mouse in *that* house,' he said excitedly, 'but what about in *this* house?

Why not keep it here, in my treehouse? They would never know I had a mouse. I could make a nice cage for it and I could smuggle food up to it. We'd have a lovely time together, me and my secret mouse!'

Pete sat down again and took from the shelf a battered little booklet. It was called *Mice and How to Keep Them*. He had bought it secretly a long while ago. He had read it from cover to cover, over and over again. Though he'd never owned one, there wasn't much Pete didn't know about handling and housing and feeding pet mice!

There were pictures of all the many different colours and markings of mice, but the grubbiest page was the one about Pink-Eyed Whites, or PEWs as they were known to proper mice experts.

Pete turned to the chapter on Housing, and studied it carefully for some time. Then he climbed down the rope ladder and went off to find his father.

13

'Dad,' he said. 'Can I make something in your workshop?'

'Depends,' Pete's father said. 'What d'you want to make?'

'Oh, just something I need for my treehouse. A kind of box.'

'To keep something in, d'you mean?'

'Yes,' said Pete truthfully.

'All right,' his father said. 'There are lots of bits of wood there, from that last set of bookshelves I made. I can't help you – I shall be out for the rest of the morning – but mind you don't hit your fingers with the hammer, and don't cut them off with the saw either.'

By the end of that morning, Pete had
built a mouse cage. Like the treehouse,
it was no beauty, but it was strongly
made. Pete had followed the instructions
in *Mice and How to Keep Them*. The cage

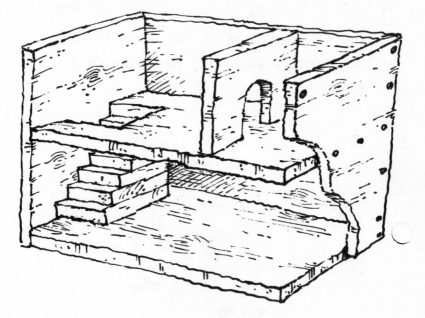

had a wire top and, inside, an upper
storey reached by a little flight of stairs:
for this upstairs part, or bedroom, he
had made a small, cosy nest box.

After a quick check to see that his father wasn't back and his mother wasn't looking, Pete climbed up into his treehouse with his mouse cage. He proudly placed it ready upon the shelf.

Much of the rest of the day was spent in preparing the other things that would be needed for his mouse.

I must have a tin to store its food in, Pete thought. *I'll need some little bowls for it to eat out of and drink from. But I can't ask Mum – she'll want to know what I want them for.*

Because it was Mouseday and the bin men didn't collect till Monday, the dustbin was full. Luckily there were some useful things in it. Pete found a good-sized old biscuit tin, and also a couple of little fish-paste jars. There was a plastic bottle too – for water – and a large polythene bag, just right for keeping sawdust in.

By bedtime, everything was prepared.
The water bottle had been filled from
the garden tap and the paste pots –
thoroughly washed – stood ready on
the sawdusted floor of the cage.

'Did you make your box?'
Pete's father asked at bedtime.
'Yes.'
'I've hardly seen anything of
him,' his mother said. 'He's been

up and down that old apple tree all afternoon.'

'That old treehouse,' his father said, with a touch of pride in his voice. 'A pretty good piece of work that, though I say so myself.'

So's my mouse cage, thought Pete, *though I say so myself. There's only one thing missing now . . .*

Chapter Two

Buying the mouse, Pete thought, *should be easy.*

First, he already had some money saved up, in a red tin shaped like a pillar box, which stood on the shelf in the treehouse.

Secondly, the local pet shop was actually on his way to school. Every weekday, Pete and his friend Dave would stop and gaze in at the animals.

Dave will have to know, Pete thought. *I can't keep it a secret from old Dave. And I can't buy the mouse on a Mouseday – Mum and Dad would ask where I was going. I'll have to get it on the way home from school.*

So, as they set out on Monday morning, Pete said to Dave, 'I'm going to buy my white mouse today.'

'With pink eyes?'
Dave said. He knew
all about Pete's
ambition. 'Are your
mum and dad going
to let you have one
at last, then?'

'No. They won't
know. It's a secret,'
said Pete. 'I'm going
to keep it in my
treehouse.'
'That's brilliant!'
Dave said.
Pete couldn't wait
for school to end.

When it did, he and Dave ran all the way to the pet shop. Inside, Pete looked around at the rabbits and the guinea pigs, the hamsters and the gerbils – until at last he saw in a corner a large cage with a number of mice running

about inside it. Some were black, some were black and white, and some were gingery. But there was no white mouse with pink eyes.

'Oh no!' groaned Pete. He felt so disappointed.

The pet-shop man came round the counter.

'What's the matter, sonny?' he said.

'Are these all the mice you've got?' asked Pete.

'Yes. Why?'

'I wanted a PEW.'

'A pew?' said the pet-shop man. 'That's something you sit on in church.'

'No,' said Pete. 'It stands for Pink-Eyed White.'

'Is that a fact?' said the pet-shop man. 'Well, in that case, I think you're in luck. I seem to remember there's one of those left.' He opened the lid of the cage.

In one corner was a big nest – a ball made of shavings and bits of straw and newspaper. The man opened it up with a finger.

Inside were some mice. One of them, Pete saw with a thrill, was a PEW!

'Did you want a buck or a doe?' the pet-shop man asked.

'I don't mind,' Pete said, 'but I'd sooner have a doe.'

The man picked up the white mouse gently, holding it by the root of its tail.

'It *is* your lucky day,' he said. 'This one's a doe.'

'Oh, good!' said Pete. He knew, from *Mice and How to Keep Them*, that it was only the bucks that smelled.

The booklet also said that mice like canary seed, so he bought a packet of that too, and the pet-shop man provided a special little cardboard box for Pete to carry the PEW home in.

When they reached Pete's gate, he said to Dave, 'Can you go and ring the

bell and then, when Mum comes, talk to her for a bit? I don't want her to see me getting up into the treehouse with this lot.'

'What shall I talk about?' said Dave.

'Oh, I don't know. Anything. Just keep her busy till I get back.'

So Dave rang the bell and, when Pete's mum came to the front door, he said, 'Hello.'

'Hello, Dave,' said Pete's mum.
'Where's Pete?'

'Who?' said Dave.

'Pete.'

'Oh, Pete,' said Dave.

'Yes. Didn't he walk back from school with you?'

'School?' said Dave.

'Yes.'

'Oh,' said Dave. 'School. Yes. He did.'

'Well, where is he?'

'Who?' said Dave.

'Oh, don't start that again,' said Pete's mum. 'Where is Pete?'

At that moment Dave saw his friend running back across the lawn, making a thumbs-up sign.

'Oh, there's Pete!' said Dave to Pete's mum. 'I've got to go. Goodbye.'

'Where've you been, Pete?' asked his mother.

'In my treehouse.'

'Well, I don't know what's up with your friend Dave. He comes and rings the bell and then talks a lot of rubbish. I couldn't get any sense out of him.'

'He's like that, old Dave is,' said Pete. 'Can I have a biscuit, Mum?'

'Can't you wait till teatime?'

'I'm hungry.'

'Oh, all right.'

When he got back to the treehouse, Pete put his PEW in the mouse cage.

He filled one pot with birdseed and the other with water.

The white mouse hurried around her home, examining everything with twitching whiskers. She climbed the stairs to her bedroom and inspected the bedding in the nest box.

When she came downstairs again, Pete offered her a little bit of biscuit. She took it in her small pink paws and began to nibble at it.

You look quite at home already, Pete thought. *But you need a name. What shall I call you?*

The white mouse stared, rather short-sightedly, at him out of her large pink eyes.

Some biscuits, like Digestives or Rich Tea, have their names written on them. Pete was just about to eat the

rest of this one when he saw the name
on it:

'That's it!' Pete said to his PEW.
'You're Nice!'

Chapter Three

Some days later Pete's mum said to her husband, 'I'm a bit worried about Pete.'

'Why?' asked Pete's dad.

'This week he's spent every spare minute up that apple tree. He's got all his toys and books in his bedroom, yet he's always in that treehouse.

'And he talks to himself up there. I heard him when I was gardening yesterday.'

'Probably had his friend Dave with him.'

'No. I thought that, but I could see Dave over the fence, playing in his own garden. And that's another thing – Dave came to our door last Monday talking a lot of rubbish. And it was just the same with Pete. I heard him saying, "Nice. Nice. Who's a good Nice?" What sense does that make?'

'I shouldn't worry,' Pete's dad said. 'He's just playing some game.'

'And another thing,' said Pete's mum. 'He seems to be eating so

much nowadays. He's always asking
me for biscuits, and yesterday I
caught him with a handful of cornflakes. When he saw me, he stuffed
them in his mouth. Dry cornflakes. I
ask you!'

Apart from that slip-up, Pete had
managed to smuggle all sorts of food
to Nice. As well as biscuits and
cornflakes, he tried her with a number
of other foods recommended in *Mice
and How to Keep Them* – bread, cake-
crumbs, and bits of carrot and apple

and banana. He only gave her very small amounts, of course, for she was only a very small animal. But Nice ate everything he gave her and seemed, Pete thought, to be growing quite fat.

She had also grown very tame. Pete would take her out of her cage and sit in his chair, and she would climb all over him, running up his arm and on to his shoulder and tickling his neck with her whiskers.

At the end of the next week, Pete and Dave were walking back from school together. It was very windy – a southwesterly gale was forecast – and they battled along with their heads down.

'How's the mouse?' shouted Dave.

'She's fine!' yelled Pete.

'Your mum and dad still haven't found out?'

'No! They never will!'

Later, Pete climbed the rope ladder to give Nice her supper. The wind was stronger now and the branches of the old apple tree were whipping about. The treehouse creaked a bit in the gathering storm.

Pete lay in bed that Friday night, listening to the wind howling outside. For a while he worried a little bit about Nice, in her cage in the treehouse in the apple tree, but then he fell asleep.

Because it was a Mouseday morning, he slept late and, by the time he woke, the wind had dropped. But when he looked out of his bedroom window, it was to see a terrible sight.

The apple tree had blown down in the gale!

It lay flat, its roots exposed. Amidst its broken

branches was the wreckage of his treehouse.

Pete dressed and dashed downstairs.

'Mum! Dad!' he cried. 'My treehouse is smashed!'

'I know,' his mum said. 'I'm so sorry, Pete.'

'Good job it happened at night, otherwise you might have been in it,' his dad said. 'You could have been killed.'

Like Nice has been, thought Pete
miserably.

He walked across the lawn and
stood by the fallen tree. The
treehouse had completely
collapsed.

His father came to stand beside him, a billhook in his hand.

'What did you have in there, Pete?' he said. 'Anything of value?'

'Yes,' said Pete. *I don't want to see her dead body*, he thought. *But I can't just leave her there.*

'Let's have a look,' said his father.

He chopped away at the tangle of branches until he reached the wreck of the treehouse. He wrenched off the battered tin roof. Under it was the garden chair (smashed), Pete's pillar box (bent but with some coins still rattling in it), *Mice and How to Keep Them* (a bit bedraggled, but still all in one piece) and . . . the mouse cage.

By some miracle it seemed to be
undamaged.

'What's this?' Pete's dad said.

'My mouse cage,' said Pete.

'Mouse cage? But you haven't got a
mouse.'

'I have,' said Pete. 'Or rather, I had. I
don't want to see her, Dad. Can you
bury her for me, please?'

He turned away.

His father opened the lid of the cage.

'Bury her?' he said. 'I don't think I'd better, Pete. She seems to be as right as rain.' He bent his head and sniffed. 'Funny,' he said. 'She doesn't smell at all.'

By the end of that Mouseday, everything had been explained and everything had been arranged. There could be no rebuilding of the treehouse – and there was no other tree in the garden. Pete was to be allowed to keep his mouse cage on the workbench in the garage.

'Just so long as I don't have to come anywhere near it,' his mother said.

'It doesn't smell,' his dad said. 'But one mouse is enough, Pete. You're not to go buying any more mice. Promise?'

'I promise,' Pete said.

Last thing that Mouseday evening, Pete went to the garage to make sure that Nice was all right.

He opened the cage, expecting to
see her come running downstairs for
her supper, but there was no sign of
her. Pete raised the lid of the little nest
box.

Inside was his PEW.
But she was not alone.

With her were six blind, fat, hairless babies.

'Nice!' said Pete softly. 'Oh, very nice indeed!'

Titus
Rules OK

Dick King-Smith

Illustrated by John Eastwood

CHAPTER ONE

In an armchair in the great high-
ceilinged drawing room sat a woman
surrounded by dogs. Some sat in other
chairs, some on the hearthrug, one, the
youngest and not much more than a
pup, on the woman's lap.

All the dogs were of the same breed.
All of them looked up as the door of
the room was opened by a tallish man

with a strong nose and receding hair and rather bristly eyebrows, who strode in with a military gait that suggested he might once have been a soldier, or perhaps a sailor.

At sight of him, the youngest dog jumped off the woman's lap and rushed

forward, getting between the man's
legs and almost tripping him up.

The bristly
eyebrows
came
together
in a frown.
'Good
heavens,
Madge!'
said the
man
angrily. 'Do
we have to have these fat
little brutes under our feet
all the time?'

The woman rose to
her full height (which
was not very great).

Unlike her husband, she was plump and had thick grey hair set in neat permanent waves.

Like him, she looked angry. 'There would be no problem if you looked where you were going,' she said in a high voice, 'and I'll thank you not to refer to my dogs as fat little brutes. They are not fat. They simply have short legs, like all corgis.'

Husband and wife stood glowering at one another in that grumpy way

that long-married people sometimes do, but before anything else could be said, there was a knock on the door and into the drawing room came a footman carrying a tray. This he placed upon a table before withdrawing, backwards.

Once the door was closed, the tallish man said, 'You feed 'em too much, Madge, that's the trouble.'

'That is your opinion, Philip,' said the Queen icily, 'which I should be glad if you would keep to yourself. Do you want a cup of coffee?'

'No, thanks, I fancy something stronger,' the man said, and he withdrew, frontwards. The Queen poured herself a cup of coffee, and then, taking from the tray a plate of biscuits, proceeded to

feed them to the corgis. 'Custard creams, my dears,' she said, smiling. 'Your favourites.' And she gave an extra one to the youngest corgi. 'Not your fault,' she said to him. 'He wasn't looking where he was going.'

Later, when the Queen had finished her coffee and left the room, the mother of the youngest corgi jumped into her chair, warm from the imprint of the Royal bottom, and her son scrambled up beside her.

His name was Titus, and like all young creatures, he was curious about everything. It was the first time he had been allowed into the drawing room of the Castle, and also the first time he had met the Queen's husband.

'Mum,' he said. 'Who was that man?'

'The Queen's husband,' his mother replied.

' "Philip", she called him,' said Titus.

'Yes. He's Prince Philip, the Duke of Edinburgh.'

'Oh,' said Titus. 'They didn't seem to like each other much.'

'I think they do,' said his mother. 'Their barks are worse than their bites.'

'Oh,' said Titus. 'Mum, you told me she's called Queen Elizabeth the Second.'

'Yes.'

'What happened to the First?'

'Died. A long time ago.'

'Oh,' said Titus. 'But, Mum, if her name's Elizabeth, why does Prince Philip call her Madge?'

'It's his nickname for her,' his mother said. 'Short for Majesty.'

Chapter Two

The door of the great drawing room now opened once again, and in came the footman to collect the tray on which stood the two cups and saucers, the coffee pot, and the plate that had held the biscuits.

The footman inspected the tray. One cup had been used, he saw, one

not, and, picking up the coffee pot, he found that it was still half full. He grinned.

'Ta very much, ma'am,' he said. 'Plenty left for me. But surely you've never scoffed all those custard creams? I could have done with a couple.'

Then he looked around the room and saw ten pairs of bright eyes watching him from various chairs or from the rug before the blazing fire. Ten pink tongues licked ten pairs of lips and ten stumps of tails wagged hopefully.

'Of course!' said the footman. 'I should have known. It wasn't her that ate 'em, it was you greedy little fatties. Treats you better than she treats old Phil, or Charlie, or the rest of 'em, she does. Pity you don't live out in the Far

East. They eat dogs out there. You lot would make a proper banquet.' And he picked up the tray.

When he had left the room, 'Mum,' said Titus. 'Who was that man?'

'Just a footman,' his mother replied.

'Footman?' said Titus. 'What was wrong with his feet?'

'Nothing, dear,' said his mother.

'A footman is one of the servants in the Castle – there are lots of them.'

'What's a servant?'

'Someone who looks after you, does whatever he or she is told, fetches and carries, just like that footman brought the tray for the Queen and the Duke.'

'But, Mum,' said Titus. 'Why couldn't they fetch their own coffee and biscuits?'

'Oh goodness me, no, Titus!' said his mother. 'That would never do. The Queen and Prince Philip have to be

looked after. They're not expected to work. When you get a little older, you'll realize that Queen Elizabeth is the most important person in the land. No one is more important than she is, at least no other human being.'

Titus cocked his ears. 'If I'm reading you right, Mum,' he said, 'you're saying that there's an animal that's more important than the Queen?'

'Several animals,' said his mother.

'What sort?'

'Pembrokeshire corgis.'

'Us, d'you mean?'

'Yes, Titus,' replied his mother. 'The Queen, you see, may be responsible for the welfare not just of her family but of all the citizens of the United Kingdom and  her realms overseas. But, in her eyes, it is our welfare that is at the top of her priorities and most important to her. She is our servant.'

'Gosh!' said Titus. 'D'you mean she'll do whatever we tell her to?'

'Certainly,' said his mother.

'If I told her to do something, she'd do it, would she, Mum?'

'If you told her in the right way.'

'How d'you mean?'

'Politely. Her Majesty does not like being barked at or yapped at. You'll have noticed that just now, when she dished out the biscuits, we all kept as quiet as mice. Any time you want a biscuit, just go and sit quite silently in front of the Queen and gaze up into her eyes with a pleading look.

'And don't ever be tempted to lift a paw and scratch at the Royal legs. A couple of years ago one of your cousins laddered Her Majesty's stockings. Never seen him since.'

'Where did he go?'

'He was sent to the Tower of London.'

'To be killed?'

'No, no, he was given to one of the warders. But the family felt the disgrace keenly.'

'The Royal Family?' asked Titus.

'No, no, our family,' said his mother. 'And one other thing, Titus, while I think of it. If ever you're taken short . . .'

'Taken short?'

'Yes, you know, if you need to, um, cock your leg, or, er, do your business, there is a proper way of going about it if the Queen is in the room. If it's anyone else, it doesn't matter, you can yap your head off or scratch at the door. But if it's

the Queen, this is the correct form. You walk to the door – no running, mind, just walk – and sit in front of it and give a little whine – no barking, mind – and you look back at Her Majesty, and then she'll hurry to let you out.'

'One thing she does *not* like and that's any sort of accident, on the carpets, say, or against the leg of a chair. Our servant she may be, but it's important to treat servants right if you want them to look after you well.'

Perhaps because his mother had just been talking about it, Titus suddenly felt that he did indeed need to do something very badly. How awful, he thought, if on this, his first time in the great drawing room at Windsor Castle, he should offend their servant the Queen by doing it, not on a chair leg, for he had not yet learned to cock his own leg, but on the carpet. Her Majesty would never forgive him!

'Mum!' he cried. 'I need a wee!'

Titus's mother, whose registered name was Lady Priscilla of Windsor but who was always called Prissy by Her Majesty, immediately began to bark loudly.

'Mayday! Mayday!' she cried to the other corgis in the room.

'What's up, Prissy?' they all asked.

'It's not what's up,' replied Prissy. 'It's what will be down unless we hurry. Titus needs to go outside, sharpish. Sound the alarm!' And at this all the other eight dogs began to bark at the tops of their voices.

Quickly the door of the drawing room was opened and in came a footman. Titus could see that it was not the same one that had come in before to fetch the tray, for that one had had fair curly hair, whereas this one had straight black hair and, as well, a strip of black hair between his nose and his mouth.

By now, Titus was whining in his distress, and the footman, instantly sizing up the situation, picked him up, hurried away down a corridor, opened a side door and popped the puppy down on the beautifully mown green grass of a lawn outside.

Thankfully Titus squatted down and did an enormous puddle.

CHAPTER THREE

'*What* a good boy!' said a voice from somewhere high above, and man and dog looked up to see the Queen leaning out of an upstairs window.

The black-moustached footman snapped to attention at sight of Her Majesty, while Titus wagged his rump on seeing the woman who, Mum had told him, was their servant.

'Leave the puppy there, John,' called the Queen. 'I'm coming right down,' and in a few moments she came out of the door on to the lawn, and bent down to stroke Titus and pat him and rub the roots of his ears, something that he found very pleasant.

'Lucky for you that you didn't do all that on my carpets,' said the Queen. 'You would have been a most unpopular pup.' Then she picked Titus up and held him

 before her face and looked into his eyes.

Most animals, dogs included, cannot bear the direct stare of a human being for long and will look away. But Titus stared back into the Royal eyes, flattening his ears with pleasure and wrinkling his lips in a sort of grin. *She seems nice, this Queen person*, he thought, and at that instant Her Majesty spoke to him once again.

'Titus, my boy,' said the Queen, 'I have a funny feeling that you are going to be a very special dog.'

At that moment there came another voice, a deep voice, from the upstairs window, and Titus looked up to see the Duke of Edinburgh leaning out.

'Telephone, Madge!' he called.

'Well, answer it, Philip, can't you?'

'I have done. It's for you.'

'I'm busy,' replied the Queen, continuing to stroke Titus. 'Who is it, anyway?'

'It's the Prime Minister.'

'Bother!' said the Queen. 'One wishes sometimes,' she said to Titus as she carried him upstairs, 'that one was not continually pestered by politicians ringing one up in one's own home. I daresay you'd be surprised to know, for instance, that what is called the Queen's

Speech is not mine at all. The whole thing's written by *my* government, which actually isn't mine anyway. I tell you, Titus, being Queen is a dog's life.'

Back in the great drawing room, Prissy was getting worried. 'Titus has been gone an awful long time,' she said to the others. 'I hope he's not got into any trouble.'

In reply, the bitches among the corgis said helpful things like 'Of course not,

dear, he'll be back in a minute, you'll see,' and the dogs made unhelpful remarks such as 'Ah well, boys will be boys,' and 'Let's hope the Prince of Wales doesn't come visiting with those terriers of his – they won't half knock the lad about.'

So it was with great relief that at last Prissy saw the door open and the Queen enter, carrying Titus, and she ran

forward whining anxiously. The Queen put the puppy down on the carpet, and his mother licked his ear.

'Where have you been all this time?' she asked him. 'Mummy's been worrying.'

'I've been with our servant,' Titus said.

'Our servant? Oh – oh, you mean Her Majesty?'

'Yes.'

'I'm sorry, Prissy,' the Queen said. 'I would have brought him back sooner, but I had to answer a phone call, and a very long phone call it was too. Politicians are all the same, they love the sound of their own voices.' She rang a bell and another footman appeared, this time a red-headed one.

'Biscuits, please, Patrick,' she said.

'Yes, Your Majesty,' said the footman. 'What kind, ma'am?'

'Custard creams. Oh, and two chocolate digestives.'

The Queen sat down in her armchair, and when the biscuits came she fed the custard creams to Prissy and the other eight adult dogs, but offered nothing to Titus.

What about me? he thought, and he moved towards the Royal legs. *Mustn't scratch at 'em,* he thought to himself, *I*

might ladder the Royal stockings. But I would like to know if there are any biscuits left on that plate, and in an effort to see, he sat bolt upright on his fat little bottom, his front paws held out imploringly before him.

'That,' said the Queen, 'is an extremely clever thing to do. Never before have I had a corgi that could manage that trick – they always fall over backwards. Now something that my great-great-grandmother Queen Victoria was fond of saying was "We are not amused." But I must tell you, Titus, that we *are* amused.' And she broke the two chocolate digestives into pieces and carefully fed them to the young corgi who, had either of them known it, was destined to become the most famous dog in the land.

Chapter Four

Ever since she was a small girl – then of course known as Princess Elizabeth – the Queen had always been surrounded by corgis. The Royal Family had many other dogs of many other sorts at Buckingham Palace, at Windsor Castle, at Sandringham, at Balmoral in Scotland. But corgis had always been the favourite breed.

Not that the Queen had a particular favourite among them, for she treated them all equally, though she might have admitted to a rather special liking for Lady Priscilla of Windsor, the senior member of the present pack. Prissy had had many puppies in her life, but the birth of her last litter had been a time of high drama. Perhaps because of her rather advanced age, the whelping was a difficult one, and an operation was needed to try to save the unborn pups. Three did not survive. One, Titus, did.

From the moment of his birth the Queen took an interest in this, the only surviving child of this last litter of her dear Prissy, which explains why he had been allowed into the great drawing room of the Castle at a much earlier age than puppies usually were.

Who knows what might have happened had Titus, so young and untrained, puddled on the carpet. But he hadn't. Instead he had asked to go out, and he had done it on the lawn, and the Queen had seen him do it. Later, what's more, he had sat bolt upright on his bottom before her, something no corgi of hers had ever done before.

'This last puppy of yours is quite a character,' said the Queen to Prissy. 'Not that I believe in favouritism, of course.' But it was not long before a great many people in the Castle, from the three footmen, fair-haired, black-moustached, red-headed, to such an august person as the Comptroller of

Her Majesty's Household, noticed that, wherever the Queen went, she was now always accompanied by one particular young corgi.

Sometimes he followed at her heels, sometimes she followed at his, but it

was soon plain to everyone that, though the Queen was on record as saying that she didn't believe in having favourites, she now had one.

Even her husband noticed. Prince Philip, though fond of dogs in general, did not particularly like corgis. 'Always tripping me up,' he would say. Now, looking carefully at Titus at teatime one day, he asked, 'I say, Madge, isn't that the little brute that nearly had me over a while ago?'

'Yes,' said the Queen, 'and he's not a brute and you should look where you're going.'

'Charles's blasted little terriers are bad enough,' said the Duke, 'but at least they're nippy enough to get out of the way. Whereas corgis are just

designed for tripping people up, bumbling about like they do, fat little beasts. Any more tea in that pot, Madge?'

When the Queen had poured her husband's tea, she took a sugar lump

from the bowl and held
it out before Titus,
who sat straight up
on his bottom, eyes
fixed upon the treat.

'Never seen one of 'em do that
before,' said Prince Philip.

'Clever, aren't you, Titus?' said the Queen, and she gave him the sugar lump.

'"Titus", is he?' said the Duke. 'Where are the rest of 'em then, Madge?'

'Oh, they're somewhere around,' replied the Queen.

'This one's a bit special then, is he?'

'You know I don't have favourites, Philip,' said the Queen. 'It's just that Titus is an only child, and Prissy's last one at that because I shan't breed from her again, not at her age.'

The Duke of Edinburgh drained his cup and stood up. 'Be nice if you didn't breed from any of 'em any more, Madge,' he said. 'That way they'd all die out and I could walk around without falling over 'em. Just hang on to that Titus till I'm out of the room.'

Left alone, the Queen rang for a footman to take away the tea things, and when he had done so (it was the black-moustached one), she picked up Titus and sat him on her lap.

'My husband,' she said to him, 'is not the easiest person in the world to get on with.'

'I mean, I'm fond of him, as I am of my daughter and my three sons, but I'm probably happiest when I'm alone with my dogs.'

She looked into Titus's eyes and, once again, he stared back into hers with that confident gaze of his.

'In fact,' said the Queen, 'I'm possibly happiest when I'm alone with you.'

Chapter Five

Hardly were the words out of the Royal mouth than there came a knock on the door. It was not the discreet knock that the footmen usually gave but a loud *rat-a-tat-tat*.

'Bother!' said the Queen to Titus. 'Who can that be?' and she called, 'Come in!'

The door opened and in came the tall distinguished figure of the Comptroller of the Household. He bowed.

'Oh, good afternoon, Sir Gregory,' said the Queen. 'What can we do for you?'

Is that the Royal 'we', thought the Comptroller, *or does she mean herself and the dog?* 'Forgive the intrusion, ma'am,' he said, 'but the Prince of Wales has just telephoned my office. He is passing through on his way from Highgrove to London and should be here very shortly.'

'Thank you, Sir Gregory,' said the Queen. 'By the way, I don't think that you've met Titus.'

'Titus, ma'am?'

'Yes, this little chap, my Prissy's last child. Titus, allow me to introduce Sir Gregory Collimore. Sir Gregory – Titus.' She put the little chap down on the floor.

'How do you do, Titus?' said the Comptroller gravely, at which the young dog sat up on his bottom, paws held out before him, and Sir Gregory took hold of the right one and solemnly shook it.

'I've never known any of Your Majesty's corgis do that before, ma'am,' he said.

'Nor have we,' said the Queen.

Scarcely had the Comptroller left the room when the door opened once again,

this time without a knock, and in came
the Prince of Wales.

'Hullo, Charles,' said the Queen.

'Hullo, Mummy,' said Prince Charles,
kissing his mother, and then, 'Who's
this?' for Titus was still sitting up on his
hunkers.

'His name is Titus,' said the Queen.

'Never known any of your corgis do
that before, Mummy. My terriers can't
do that.'

'Not surprised,' said the Queen. 'Tell me, why are you going to London?'

'Regimental dinner, Mummy. I am Colonel-in-Chief of the Welsh Guards, remember?'

The Queen smiled a rather patronizing smile. 'Of course I remember, Charles,' she said. 'The most junior of the five regiments. As you no doubt remember, I happen to be Colonel-in-Chief of the Grenadiers, the most senior regiment in the Brigade of Guards.'

The Prince of Wales laughed a somewhat uneasy laugh. 'I shall have that job one day, Mummy,' he said.

'When I'm dead and gone, you mean?'

'Well, er, yes.'

'And you're King Charles the Third?'

'Well, er, yes.'

Titus was still sitting up on his bottom and the Queen bent down and spoke softly in his ear. 'He's going to have to wait an awfully long time,' she whispered. 'Specially if I live to be as old as my mum.' And she giggled.

'What's funny, Mummy?' asked Prince Charles.

'Oh just a little joke between me and Titus.'

'You talk as if he could understand what you're saying.'

'He can, Charles, he can,' said the Queen. 'Now off you go to London, there's a good boy.'

A little later, in the great drawing room of Windsor Castle, the corgis sprang to attention, ears cocked, back ends wagging, as the Queen came in, carrying Titus.

'Sorry, Prissy,' she said, putting the puppy down with his mother. 'I couldn't bring your son back earlier because I had a visit from my son.'

When she had gone out again, Prissy said to Titus, 'Which son?'

'How d'you mean, Mum?'

'Well, Her Majesty . . .'

'Our servant, you mean?'

'Yes, she has three sons. What did she call this one? Was it Edward?'

'No.'

'Was it Andrew?'

'No.'

'Then it must have been Charles.'

'Yes, that was his name.'

'He's the Prince of Wales, of course,' said Prissy.

'So he's Welsh, like us?'

'No, he's English. Prince of Wales is his title. He'll be King of England when the Queen dies.'

'He's going to have to wait an awfully long time,' said Titus.

'Whatever d'you mean?'

'Well, that's what the servant told me.'

'Oh, Titus!' said Prissy. 'What a lovely boy you are. How I do love you.'

In an upstairs sitting room Queen Elizabeth the Second was just settling down to read the Court Circular section of the *Daily Telegraph* when in came Prince Philip, Duke of Edinburgh, carrying a copy of *The Times*, open at Sport.

'Morning, Madge,' he said.

'Good afternoon, Philip,' his wife replied.

'It's nearly one o'clock.'

'Oh, is it?' said the Duke. 'What's for lunch?'

'For you,' said the Queen, 'I've no idea. I'm having mine in here, on a tray. My favourites – Marmite sandwiches and cold rice pudding with strawberry jam.'

'Ugh!' said the Duke. 'Those corgis of yours get better grub than you do. You spoil 'em, Madge, especially that puppy you're always carrying around. Anyone would think he was Heir to the Throne. Which reminds me, Collimore tells me that Charles is here.'

'He was. He's gone.'

'Oh. All right, is he?'

'He didn't say.'

'Hm,' said Prince Philip. 'Well, I must go and look for some lunch. Who knows, if I get down on all fours and wag my behind, maybe one of the footmen will bring me a nice plate of custard creams.'

CHAPTER SIX

Beyond knowing their names, Prince
Philip knew nothing of the three
footmen who came to answer any bell
that he or the Queen might ring in
Windsor Castle. When he spoke to
one of them, to give an order, it
was always in an abrupt manner,
but then that was how he spoke to
everyone.

The Queen did not know much more of them. She knew that Sidney, the one with fair curly hair, was from London, that John, black of hair and moustache, was a Scot, and that red-headed Patrick hailed from Ireland. When speaking to any of them, she was always civil, for she had been taught as a child that one should never, never be rude to servants. But of their characters she knew nothing.

The three footmen were indeed very different, one from another. Patrick was a jolly fellow, always making jokes. He had an eye for the girls, and more than one of the maids that worked in the Castle had been winked at by the red-headed footman.

Though John, a quiet, serious person, would never have dreamed of doing such a thing himself, he got on well with Patrick.

But neither the Scotsman nor the Irishman had any particular liking for fair, curly-headed Sidney, the third footman, who claimed to have been born in a rather smart part of London. He was indeed a smart-looking chap but Patrick and John somehow did not trust him too much.

Neither of them would have ever finished off any leftover coffee or biscuits, as Sidney always did, and each of them had, at one time or another, seen Sidney slip a couple of custard creams into his pocket before proceeding to the great drawing room or to one of the Queen's sitting rooms with a tray. Sidney, they agreed between themselves, was light-fingered. But they had no idea just how untrustworthy the Londoner was.

Nor had the Queen.

Until one fateful day when Sidney did something rather unwise and Titus won his spurs.

Time had flown, as it does, and Titus was now a year old, though the Queen still referred to him as 'my puppy Titus'.

'I'm not a puppy any more, am I, Mum?' he said to his mother.

'No, dear,' replied Prissy. 'You are a grown-up corgi and a very handsome one too. No wonder the servant spoils you like she does. Why, you'll be sleeping on her bed next, I shouldn't wonder.'

By now Titus knew his way around the Castle pretty well, and though he'd never actually been in the Queen's bedroom, he knew where it was. That afternoon he trotted along, through passages and corridors and up flights of stairs, until he came to its door which, rather to his surprise, was ajar. He peeped into the room and there, at the Queen's dressing table, was the fair-haired footman.

As Titus watched, Sidney picked up a silver box (a jewel case it was, could Titus have known) and opened its lid and peered inside. Something told Titus that this was wrong. The man shouldn't be there in the Royal bedroom, he felt sure, and he gave a little growl.

Sidney swung round, hastily closing the jewel case. Then, seeing Titus standing alone in the doorway, he heaved a sigh of relief. 'Blimey, you gave me a fright, you little fattie!' he said. 'I've got a good mind to kick your fat backside.' And he made a move towards Titus, who ran off,

barking. A couple of hours later, Sidney sat in the saloon bar of a backstreet Windsor pub, in company with a rather flashily dressed middle-aged man. They sat in a far corner, talking quietly over their pints.

'It'll be as easy as pie, Percy,' said Sidney. 'She hadn't even locked it.'

'You're sure it's hers, Sid?' asked the man, Percy.

'Course it's hers. It's in her bedroom. And it's crammed full of jewels. Rings, brooches, earrings, necklaces, worth a fortune they must be. Soon as I saw 'em, I thought of you, Perce. *Old Perce the fence*, I said to myself, *he'll place 'em for me*. She'll never even notice they're gone. It's a piece of cake.'

'Slow down, slow down, Sid,' said Percy. 'Nice and easy does it, you don't want to go taking too much at a time. Just pick a few things for a start, mind.'

'And we'll split what they fetch, fifty-fifty, Perce?'

'Sixty to me, Sid, forty to you. I've got to place them.'

'But I've got to nick them!'

'Piece of cake, you said.'

'Well, yes, she's gone up to Buckingham Palace with old Phil, but it's risky all the same.'

'You just go and get them, Sid,' said the fence. 'Just a few small things you can put in your pockets. I'll meet you back here later.'

And so it was that later that evening the fair-haired footman Sidney made his cautious way up to the bedroom of Her Majesty Queen

Elizabeth the Second. Because the Queen was not in residence, many of the servants, including John and Patrick, were taking time off, and even Sir Gregory Collimore had put his feet up. But there was someone who was still on duty.

The more Titus thought about what he had seen in the Queen's bedroom, the more he felt first that that footman was a bad man and second that he, Titus, must guard the servant's possessions in her absence.

He did not consult his mother about this (*I'm not a puppy any more*, he thought) but in turn made his cautious way up to Her Majesty's bedroom and crept under Her Majesty's great four-poster bed and curled up comfortably on Her Majesty's thick carpet.

If the man doesn't come back, he thought, *I'll have a jolly good sleep.*

If he does, he'll have the surprise of his life.

Which indeed Sidney did. Hardly had he opened the Royal jewel case than he heard a sudden snarl and felt a battery of sharp teeth biting into his ankle.

CHAPTER SEVEN

'GERRIMOFF! GERRIMOFF!!'

It was a passing maid who
first heard the frantic yells
coming from the Queen's
bedroom, and she ran
to tell other members
of staff, and they
alerted the officer
commanding the

Castle guard, and he telephoned the Comptroller of Her Majesty's Household. Sir Gregory arrived at the doorway of the Royal bedroom to see before him an extraordinary sight.

Inside there stood an officer of the Grenadier Guards and half a dozen guardsmen, weapons at the ready. Scattered all over the carpet, Sir Gregory could see, were rings and brooches and earrings and necklaces and a silver jewel case, open and empty. Among all these valuables Sidney the footman hopped and howled, one of his ankles held, in a bulldog grip, by a furiously growling corgi.

'Gerrimoff!' he still cried feebly, and at a signal from the officer, one of the

guardsmen laid down his rifle and knelt and managed to prise open the dog's jaws and thus release the prisoner. And a prisoner of course Sidney was destined to be, for his guilt was plain to the onlookers (and indeed his pockets were full of rings) and, in due course, to the judge.

The footman had been caught in the act of stealing the Queen's jewels, and caught, what's more, by the cunning and courage of one of Her Majesty's corgis.

After the soldiers had taken the man away to be placed in police custody, Sir Gregory Collimore went to his office to report the matter by telephone to the Queen at Buckingham Palace.

'Nabbed him, did he, Sir Gregory?' she said. 'Got him by the ankle, eh?'

'Yes, ma'am. The man's leg was quite severely lacerated, I understand.'

'Serves him right,' said the Queen. 'Which of my corgis did the deed?'

'I am told it was the one to whom Your Majesty formally introduced me, some months ago. His name, as I recall, ma'am, is Titus.'

'My Titus!' cried the Queen. 'I'll come straight back! I must reward him!'

Reward him? Sir Gregory thought to himself as he put down the phone.

What's she going to do – give him a medal? It'll have to be the DCM. (Distinguished Corgi Medal), and he left his office, smiling at his own joke.

In the Palace, the Queen put down her receiver and turned to the Duke of Edinburgh. 'Did you hear that, Philip?' she said.

'How could I hear it, Madge?' Prince Philip replied. 'You answered the phone, not me. But I gathered that one of your wretched corgis had bitten someone.'

'It was Titus. He nabbed one of the footmen. Bit him.'

'In the foot?'

'No, in the ankle. In my bedroom.'

'Why? Hadn't the man given him enough custard creams?'

'Don't be silly, Philip. He was robbing my jewel case.'

'Who, the corgi?'

'No, the footman, of course.'

'Which one?'

'Sidney.'

'Is that the fair-haired one, Madge?'

'Yes.'

'Never liked the cut of his jib,' said Prince Philip. 'Eyes too close together. And his ears – too small. Never trust a chap with small ears. Always knew he was a phoney.'

'Anyway,' said the Queen, 'we are going straight back to Windsor.'

'We?'

'I am going straight back.'

'Oh I see. It was the Royal "we".'

'Philip,' said the Queen coldly. 'We are not amused.'

As soon as she arrived back at Windsor Castle, the Queen went into the great drawing room, where all her corgis

were, as usual, gathered. All, as usual, got off armchairs and sofas and assembled around the Royal ankles, ears flattened, bottoms waggling, but on this day the Queen had eyes for one only.

'Titus!' she said. 'You are a hero!' And she tugged at a long bell pull that hung beside the fireplace.

The black-moustached footman knocked and entered.

'Custard creams, please, John,' said the Queen. 'Nine of them. Plus three chocolate digestives. And a pot of tea for me.'

CHAPTER EIGHT

As Titus grew up, he found that not everyone was easy to get on with. Always he tried hard to behave with the same politeness and good manners as his servant the Queen did. But the day came when he once more used his teeth in anger.

One particular corgi called Chum never lived up to his name because

 he wasn't very friendly to anyone, especially Titus. When Titus had first been allowed into the great drawing room, much earlier than puppies usually were, Chum had taken an instant dislike to him.

At first it was just a matter of seniority. Chum was at that time two years old, and he thought that Prissy's son was too bumptious by half. He growled and

showed his teeth whenever Titus came near.

But then, once it became obvious to all the corgis that Titus was well on the way to becoming the Queen's favourite, it was, for Chum, a matter of pure jealousy. Why should this whippersnapper be so spoiled?

For Chum, worse was to come, for after Titus's encounter with the burgling footman, the Queen broke all

her previous rules. She allowed Titus to sleep on the end of her bed at nights. Prissy, of course, was very proud when this happened, and most of the others didn't much mind, but there were some who feared that this privilege would give Titus a swelled head, and Chum was especially narked.

One day, by chance, he met Titus in a corridor, and his feelings boiled over. 'Hey, you!' he growled at Titus, who was about to pass peace-fully by. 'I want a word with you, you cocky little pup!'

'Excuse me,' said Titus politely. 'I am no longer a puppy. I am an adult corgi.'

'Adult, are you?' snarled Chum. 'Old enough to defend yourself then?'

'Defend myself?' said Titus. 'Against whom?'

'Against me,' Chum replied. 'I'm fed up to the back teeth –' and he showed them – 'with you and your airs and graces. Think yourself special, don't you? Think you're a cut above the rest of us, eh?'

'No, I don't.'

'Sleeping on the Queen's bed, eh?' went on Chum. 'How d'you get up on it, then?'

'The servant lifts me up.'

'Servant? What servant?'

'The Queen. Mum says she is our servant.'

'Oh, she says that, does she?' growled Chum. He took a pace forward, so that their noses were almost touching. 'Well, all I can say is – your mother's a silly old fool.'

This was too much for Titus. Up to that point he'd been hoping to avoid a fight with the older dog, and even thinking that it might perhaps be wise to run for it, back to the safety of the great drawing room. But to hear his beloved mother called 'a silly old fool'!

'How dare you say that!' he cried, and he sank his teeth into one of Chum's ears.

The noise of the fight rang down the long corridors, to be clearly heard by all the other corgis, by the two footmen, by the Comptroller of Her Majesty's Household, by Prince Philip, Duke of Edinburgh – and finally by Queen Elizabeth herself. All in turn hastened to the scene.

First came Prissy, loudly barking, 'Mummy's coming, darling!' and followed by the rest of the pack.

Then John of the black moustache and Patrick of the red hair came running, followed, as quickly as he could manage, by a hurrying Sir Gregory Collimore.

Then 'What the devil's going on?'
shouted a loud voice as Prince Philip
arrived. By now all the corgis had
joined in the scuffle, and both the
footmen had been nipped while
trying to break it up, and Sir Gregory,
a little dizzy from his unaccustomed
haste, had unfortunately tripped up

Prince Philip, so that both fell to the floor.

Then suddenly a high-pitched voice cried loudly, 'QUIET!' and lo, there was quiet, for not one of the corgis would have dreamed of disobeying such a Royal Command. The Queen stood, hands on hips, surveying the scene.

Several of her dogs were licking at nipped paws or torn ears, her footmen

were trying to bandage with hand-kerchiefs their sore fingers, and on the floor of the corridor sprawled the prostrate figures of her breathless Comptroller and her furious Consort.

But she had eyes for only one. 'Titus!' she called. 'Are you all right?'

CHAPTER NINE

The damage to Titus, the Queen found, was very little. Prissy and the other corgis had mostly pitched in to poor Chum, who was looking rather the worse for wear. As well as having had an ear quite badly bitten by Titus (from then on it always drooped a bit), he

had had a number of nips to nose and paws, and the Queen spent some time attending to him that evening. She also commanded the two footmen to see a doctor, and she made sure that her elderly Comptroller was none the worse for his fall.

Not till all this was done did she go to enquire after her husband. 'You didn't hurt yourself, did you, Philip?' she asked when they met in her sitting room.

'Luckily, no.'

'How did you come to fall?'

'Old Collimore tripped me up,' replied the Duke of Edinburgh. 'Wasn't his fault, it was all due to those blasted corgis of yours, Madge. I expect that one you call Titus started it. I just wish you'd get rid of the whole pack of them.'

'Get rid of them?' said the Queen.

'Yes, give 'em away to someone. Why don't you give 'em to Charles? They're Welsh, he's the Prince of Wales – send 'em all down to Highgrove. Or give 'em to Anne. Or Andrew. Or Edward. Or whatshername, the Duchess of Thingamajig, you know?'

The Queen drew herself up to her full modest height. 'Generally speaking, Philip,' she said in an icy voice, 'you do not forget yourself to this extent. May I remind you that I am Queen of England and will not be spoken to in this way. How dare you suggest that I should part with my beloved corgis!'

'Only joking, Madge,' said her husband.

'A joke,' said the Queen, 'in the poorest of taste.' And she swept out of the room.

Left to himself, Prince Philip stood, wryly regarding his reflection in a looking glass on the wall. 'Well, well,' he said.

'The old girl still packs a pretty good broadside. It's a wonder she didn't tell me to "Sit!" or "Stay!" ' He rang a bell.

Shortly, there was a knock on the door. 'Come in!' shouted the Duke, and in came the red-haired footman, two of his fingers bandaged.

The Duke looked at him thoughtfully. 'Are you married?' he asked.

'Married, Your Royal Highness?' said Patrick. 'No, sir, I am not.'

'Well, take my advice and don't bother. Or if you do, make sure that you're master in your own house. Now, get me a drink and run me a nice hot bath. I've had enough of today.'

When the Queen returned later, she found the red-haired footman on his knees, making up the fire. He sprang to his feet.

'Where is Prince Philip, Patrick?' the Queen asked.

The Duke of Edinburgh's private bathroom chanced to be immediately above that particular sitting room in Windsor Castle, and the footman instinctively gave an upward look at the ceiling as he answered, 'His Royal Highness is taking a bath, Your Majesty.'

'Thank you, Patrick,' said the Queen. 'You may leave the fire now, I'll see to it. How are your fingers, by the way?'

'Sure they're fine, ma'am, thank you, ma'am.'

'And John's had his seen to?'

'Yes, ma'am. The doctor bandaged us both up. A nasty nip he said it was,' the footman told her, and he bowed and left the room, backwards.

The Queen sat down and patted her lap and Titus jumped up on to it. 'What a dreadful business! Whoever nipped the footmen's fingers, I'm sure it wasn't you, dear boy. It was probably poor old Chum. I wonder what that rumpus was all about? Pity you can't tell me.'

Somehow Titus had a pretty good idea what the servant was saying. *I'm sure you'd understand why I went for Chum,* he thought. *You'd do the same if someone had called your mother a silly old fool.*

The Queen and her dog sat comfortably together before the fire, and before long the Royal eyes began

to close. What with one thing and another, it had been a rather exhausting day for Her Majesty, and she dozed off. Titus, too, felt tired after the fight and, as he settled happily on the Royal lap, he sleepily thought, *Now I'm a lapdog.* He was about to take a snooze when suddenly he heard a noise.

It was only a little noise, a sort of *plop*, the sound a drip of water makes. He opened his eyes and saw that there was indeed a drip of water falling on to the carpet of the sitting room. He looked up and saw another drop fall, and another, and another, until there was a steady stream of water falling from a rapidly growing patch of damp on the ceiling, that ceiling that was directly below Prince Philip's private bathroom.

CHAPTER TEN

Something's up! thought Titus. *Or rather, something's down!* He began to bark. The Royal eyes opened smartly, to see what could only now be called a waterfall. Leaping from her chair, the Queen ran for the door with Titus at her heels.

Prince Philip's bath was not the usual sort. It had belonged to his wife's great-great-grandmother, Queen

Victoria. She had been very short, so her bath was very short too, which suited the Duke of Edinburgh well, for even though he was tall, he liked to sit up in the tub. Which was just as well, for if, on that particular evening, he had been lying down in it as most people do, then the Queen would very probably have soon been referred to – as her great-great-grandmother had been – as the Widow of Windsor.

As it was, the Duke sat up in his bathwater,

a large glass of whisky in the soap dish by his side, and reflected upon the events of the day. *Madge and her wretched corgis,* he thought. *Lazy, fat, spoiled little brutes.* All the same, there was one of them with a bit of character, that one that had caught the burgling footman. What was the dog's name? Ah yes, Titus, that was it.

After a while the bathwater grew a little cool, and the Duke turned on the taps again. But then, lulled by the warm water and the whisky, he began to feel rather sleepy. His chin dropped upon his chest, and the sound of his snores mingled with the splashing of water from the two still-running bath taps.

Gradually the level in Queen Victoria's bath rose, till it reached the overflow. Then, because the overflow couldn't cope with the volume of water, it rose higher, to the rim of the bath, over the rim of the bath, and began to spill on to the floor. Through it all Prince Philip slept peacefully, till he was suddenly woken by a volley of barking coming from the room directly below. Not for nothing had the Prince served his time in the Royal Navy.

Open the seacock! he thought, and he yanked the plug out, and then with a loud shout of 'Abandon ship!' he leaped out of the bath.

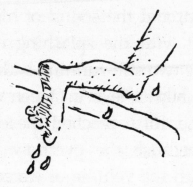

Hastily wrapping himself in a large towel, he paddled across the sodden floor. As he reached the bathroom door, it was flung open, and there stood the figure of the Queen, at her heels a single corgi.

'Sorry, Madge,' the Duke said damply. 'I dropped off to sleep in the tub. Some dog barking woke me up.'

'This dog woke you up,' replied the Queen. 'This dog, my Titus. If it hadn't been for his watchfulness, the ceiling would probably have come down on top of us. Frankly, Philip, I have to say that we are not amused.'

Then she looked again at the tall figure of her Consort, standing barefooted on the squelchy floor, clutching his damp bath towel around him, and dripping.

She began to hoot with laughter.

CHAPTER ELEVEN

Bewildered, Titus made his own way back to the great drawing room. *Humans*, he thought as he went, *I don't understand them. I mean, look at our servant just now – one minute she was angry, the next she was laughing her head off. Perhaps it's because they're Royals, maybe they're different from other people. They must be if you think about it because*

everybody else treats them quite differently. I mean, look at the footmen, they go out of the room backwards, and the maids, they curtsy, and Sir Gregory, he bows. Royal people must be very special.

I wonder if Royal dogs are too? After all, we corgis are the Queen's dogs, so maybe we're all princes and princesses. Prince Titus, how does that sound? Actually, I think I'd rather be a king among dogs. King Titus the First. Yes, that's more like it.

'Wherever have you been?' Prissy asked her son when he came into the room. 'You're all wet – your paws are soaking.'

All the other corgis gathered around Titus while he explained what had been going on.

'The bathwater came right through the ceiling, you say?' Prissy asked.

'Yes, right down into the Queen's sitting room.'

'But why,' asked one of the other dogs, 'hadn't Prince Philip turned the taps off?'

'He went to sleep in the bath,' Titus replied.

'And she was angry with him?' asked someone else.

'Yes, very.'

'But then she started laughing, you say?' said another.

'Yes,' said Titus. 'I don't understand people. They don't seem to act normally, like dogs do.'

'Well, dogs get angry sometimes, don't they?' said Prissy. 'You did, with Chum.'

'That wasn't anything to laugh at,' growled Chum, and he continued, unsuccessfully, to try to lick his injured ear.

'Anyway,' said Prissy, 'if I've got the story right, it was your barking that woke both of them up.'

es,' said Titus.

'You seem to be making quite a name for yourself, my son,' Prissy said. 'First catching a burglar, and now giving the alarm and saving the situation. What next? I wonder. If you keep on like this, you won't only be sleeping on the Queen's bed, you'll be eating off her plate, I shouldn't be surprised.'

At that moment the Queen came into the room. All the dogs crowded

around her, and she gave each a pat and a special stroking to Chum ('How's your poor ear feeling, old boy?') and to Prissy ('How does it feel to be the mother of a hero, eh?').

Then she rang the bell, and when the black-moustached footman came in, she said, 'Take all the dogs out on to the lawn, please, John.' When that had been done, the Queen ordered custard creams all round (with an extra chocolate digestive for the hero) and when those had been eaten, she said, 'Right, everybody, bedtime!' and nine corgis settled themselves comfortably in armchairs and on sofas, while the tenth and youngest followed Her Majesty as she made her way to the State Bedroom.

Once she herself was comfortably settled, the Queen turned out her bedside light. She yawned. Then she wiggled her toes against the warm shape that lay on the end of her bed. 'G'night, Titus,' she said sleepily. 'I may be a queen among my people but you're a king among my dogs.'

Chapter Twelve

For most of his long life Sir Gregory
Collimore had been in the service of
the Royal Family, and for many years
now he had been Comptroller of the
Queen's Household at Windsor Castle.
But for most of his long life, Sir Gregory
had had a very bad habit. He smoked
cigarettes, lots of them, every day. And
one day, before Titus was so very much

older, Sir Gregory's bad habit almost caused a disaster.

It happened like this.

The Comptroller came out of his office, closing the door behind him, and made his rather slow way along the corridors towards his private quarters. In an ashtray on his office desk lay the end of his latest cigarette. Maybe he had forgotten to stub it out, maybe he hadn't stubbed it out properly, but it was still alight.

Then a little puff of wind came in through the open

window, and the cigarette end rolled off the ashtray and on to some papers that lay on the desk. By a lucky chance Titus was on his way from the Queen's sitting room to the great drawing room, to pay a visit to his mother and all the other corgis, when he smelled smoke. A dog's sense of smell is many, many

times sharper than a human's, and it was immediately plain to Titus that something was burning.

That was nothing unusual, for there were dozens of fires of coal or logs all over Windsor Castle. But this smell, Titus's nose told him, was not of coal or logs. It was of burning paper. Just as he had been in the matter of the burgling footman and the overflowing bath, Titus was immediately on the alert. Something, he knew, was wrong. Someone must be told about it.

At that precise moment Prince Philip came in sight, marching along the corridor, and Titus turned and ran towards him. Now, though he cordially disliked almost all his wife's dogs, there was something about this particular one that had rather taken the Duke's fancy, and he said (in quite a pleasant voice), 'Hullo there, Titus. What's the hurry?'

By now the smell of burning paper was very strong in the dog's little nose, though it had not yet reached the man's much bigger one, and in his anxiety Titus began to tug at the Royal trouser turn-ups.

'Belay that!' growled the Duke of Edinburgh. 'What the devil d'you think you're playing at?' But Titus continued to tug and to whine and then to run a little way towards the burning smell and then back, again and again, till at last the Duke got the message and followed. Now he too smelled the smoke and broke into a run. Titus ran directly to the door of Sir Gregory Collimore's office and scratched at it, and the Duke flung it open, to see a great many papers burning merrily away on the Comptroller's desk, itself now alight. Now was the moment when Prince Philip's naval training came into play.

'England expects every man will do his duty!' he shouted, and his duty indeed he did, regardless of his own safety. There was no fire party to be summoned nor fire hoses to be brought to bear, as there would have been on board ship. But the Duke saw immediately that, in the absence of water, the growing fire must quickly be smothered. But with what? There was no handy rug – the floor of the Comptroller's office was close-carpeted – but on the wall behind there hung above the burning desk a large picture, a portrait of Sir Gregory Collimore in full ceremonial dress.

Quickly the Duke of Edinburgh yanked the portrait from its hangings and somehow found the strength (for it was very heavy) to slam the painted Sir Gregory down upon the fire, face first, and thus to extinguish the flames.

'Phew!' he said, mopping his Royal brow. 'That could have been very nasty, Titus. In fact, if it hadn't been for you, it *would* have been very nasty. Come on, old chap, we'll go and tell Madge. This will be worth a good few custard creams to you. Might even get one myself if I'm lucky.'

When the Queen was told, her first thought was for her favourite. 'You're not hurt, Titus, are you?' she said. 'You haven't burned your paws?'

'I put the fire out, you know, Madge,' said the Duke in a rather hurt voice. He held out his hands, black from his firefighting efforts. 'And my paws are dirty.'

'Yes, yes, Philip, so you said. But it was my clever little Titus that gave the alarm again.' She rang for a footman. When the custard creams came, she began to feed them to Titus, disregarding the ten pairs of eyes (nine corgis and a Duke) that were watching hungrily.

'He's a king among dogs, don't you think, Philip?' she said.

'Well, I'm a prince among men.'

'Oh, all right,' said the Queen. 'You can have one if you like.'

CHAPTER THIRTEEN

Later that day Queen Elizabeth the Second and her husband Prince Philip, Duke of Edinburgh, sat watching television together, as many elderly couples do. This couple, however, seldom did, their tastes in viewing being very different, but now something seemed to have made them more companionable. They sat side by side upon a sofa, between them the plump brown body of Titus, and the Queen suddenly noticed that her husband was absently fondling the dog's big ears.

'Never seen you do that before, Philip,' she said.

'Do what?'

'Make a fuss of any of my corgis.'

'Hm,' said the Duke. 'Well, as you know, Madge, they aren't my favourite animals. But I've taken rather a shine to this chap. Remarkable little beast, really.'

The Queen put a hand to her face to hide a smile. They were watching a documentary about vandalism in inner-city areas and there was a shot of a public building, its wall liberally daubed with graffiti in large white letters. Some of the words were rather rude, at which the Queen looked disapproving and the Duke guffawed.

Many of the messages had something in common.

Man Utd rules OK.
T. Blair rules OK.
Jeremy Paxman
rules OK.
Posh and Becks rule OK.

and so on and so forth.

'What's all that?' asked the Queen testily. 'I'm the only person who rules. OK?'

'I know, Madge, I know,' said Prince Philip, and he put a hand to his face to hide a grin.

'How do they write these stupid messages?' asked the Queen.

'With spraycans of paint, I believe,' her husband replied. 'Kind of an aerosol gadget – you just press a button and it squirts out.'

'Ridiculous!' said the Queen. 'Vandalism like that is so mindless. Imagine doing such a thing.'

'I can't imagine you doing it, Madge,' the Duke said.

'As if I would!' snorted the Queen. That night, as she settled herself for sleep, she addressed the warm shape lying against her feet at the bottom of her bed. 'As if I would, Titus,' she said, and after a moment a small smile flickered across the Royal features.

Next morning she sent for one of her Ladies-in-Waiting. 'Would you be good enough,' she said to her, 'to do a little shopping for me?'

'Of course, ma'am,' replied the Lady-in-Waiting. 'What was it that you wanted?'

'I think they're called spraycans,' the Queen said. 'They squirt paint. I want to decorate something.'

The Lady-in-Waiting looked puzzled. 'Er, what colour would you like, ma'am?' she asked.

'Golden, please.'

That night the soldiers on guard at Windsor Castle patrolled as usual around the various buildings, pausing beneath the windows of the Queen's sitting room, opposite which, on the other side of a courtyard, was a large blank wall. Not until they had marched out of sight did a shadowy figure emerge, carrying an object, and approach the wall.

Next morning Prince Philip was woken early by his wife, on whom Titus was, as usual, in attendance.

'Come and have a look, Philip,' said the Queen. 'We want to show you something.'

Grumbling, the Duke followed her into her sitting room. 'Show me what?' he growled.

'Have a look outside,' said the Queen, and he went to the window and looked out, and there on the wall opposite was written in huge golden capital letters:

'Good grief!' said the Duke. 'Who did that?'

'I did.'

'You did, Madge?'

'Yes,' said the Queen, fondly stroking her favourite corgi. 'I told you, Phil, he's a king among dogs, aren't you, Titus?'

Prince Philip shook his head in wonderment. 'Madge, old girl,' he said. 'How could you do such a thing?'

'With this, of course,' replied the Queen, producing the spraycan. 'It was

such fun, Phil. In fact, with all due respect to Great-great-grandmama, we are quite definitely amused.' And then they both burst out laughing.

The Jenius

Dick King-Smith

Illustrated by Ann Kronheimer

CHAPTER ONE
GUINEA PIGS AREN'T STUPID

'If I was the Queen,' Judy said, 'I wouldn't have corgis.'

'What sort of dogs would you have, Judy?' said her teacher.

The class were talking about pets and which were their favourites.

'I wouldn't have dogs at all.'

'What would you keep then,' said Judy's teacher, 'if you were the Queen?'

195

'Guinea pigs,' said Judy.

Everybody burst out laughing and Judy went very red.

'They're my favourite animals,' she said defiantly. 'If I was the Queen I'd keep lots of them.'

'In hutches, you mean?'

'No. In Buckingham Palace.'

'But, Judy,' said her teacher, 'wouldn't it look rather odd if someone very important came to call, like, say, the President of the United States of America, and the Queen – I mean you – said "Do take a seat, Mr President," and

there was a guinea pig lying in the armchair?'

'And there'd be messes all over the carpet,' someone said.

'And the President would step in them,' said someone else.

Everybody giggled.

'My guinea pigs would be house-trained,' muttered Judy, close to tears.

'Palace-trained, you mean,' said a voice, and now there was so much sniggering that the teacher said 'That's enough, children.'

She put her hand on Judy's shoulder and said: 'It's a nice idea, but even if you were the Queen you wouldn't be able to train a guinea pig like you can train a dog. Only certain animals are intelligent enough to be taught things by humans, and I'm afraid guinea pigs are not among them. They're dear little creatures, Judy, but they haven't got a lot of brains.'

CHAPTER TWO
AN UNEXPECTED ARRIVAL

'You *have* got a lot of brains,' said Judy.

As always, she had run down to the shed at the bottom of the garden the moment she arrived home from school, to see her own two guinea pigs. One was a reddish rough-haired boar called Joe and the other was a smooth-coated white sow by the name of Molly. Judy had had them ever since her sixth birthday, nearly two years ago now, and they were very dear to her. Her only regret was that, surprisingly, they had never had babies.

'You *have* got brains,' she said, 'I'm sure of it. It's just that no one's ever taught you to use them. Now, if I'd had you when you were tiny, I bet I could have taught you lots of things. If only you'd had children of your own. I'd have chosen one of them and kept it and really trained it, from a very early age. I bet I could have done.'

As usual, the guinea pigs responded to the sound of her voice by beginning a little conversation of their own. First Joe made a grumbling sort of chatter (which meant 'Molly, you're as lovely now as the day I first set eyes on you'), and then Molly gave a short shy squeak (which meant 'Oh, Joe, you say the nicest things!').

Then they both squealed long and loudly at Judy. She knew what that noise meant. They were telling her to cut the cackle and dish up the grub.

'Greedy old things,' she said, and she picked up the white one, Molly.

'Molly!' said Judy. 'You look awfully fat. Whatever's the matter with you?'

Molly didn't reply. Joe grunted in a self-satisfied sort of way.

'I'll have to put you on a diet,' said Judy firmly, 'starting tomorrow.'

But next morning, when she went to feed the guinea pigs, the white one, she found, looked quite different.

'Molly!' said Judy. 'You look awfully thin. Whatever's the matter with you?'

This time they both answered, Molly with a series of small happy squeaks and Joe with a low, proud grumble, as they moved aside to show what had

happened. There between them was a single, very large, baby guinea pig, the child of their old age. It was partly white and smooth like its mother and partly red and rough like its father.

To Judy's delight it stumbled forward on feet that seemed three sizes too big, until it bumped the wire of the hutch-front with its huge head. Its eyes were very bright and seemed to shine with intelligence. Then it spoke a single word in guinea-pig language. Anyone could have told it meant 'Hullo!'

'Oh!' said Judy. 'Aren't you beautiful!'

'He gets it from his mother,' chattered Joe in the background.

'And aren't you brainy!'

'He takes after his dad,' squeaked Molly.

Judy stared into the baby's eyes.

'You,' she said, 'are going to be the best-trained, most brilliant guinea pig in the whole world. And you're going to start lessons right away. Now then. Sit!'

Of course, when you're only a few hours old, standing can be tiring, but was that the reason why Joe and Molly's son immediately sat down?

CHAPTER THREE
TRAINING

That night, before she went to bed, Judy wrote the great news in her diary. She was very faithful about putting something in it every day, even if sometimes it was only a bit about the weather. But that Joe and Molly should have had a baby – that was great news and deserved a lot of space.

JUDY'S DIARY PRIVIT.

JUNE 10th: Great Surprise! Molly had a baby! Found him first thing this morning and I am going to train him. Alreddy he sits when he is told. He is briliant. He is mostly white like Molly but he has a sort of main like a horse running

all down his back that is reddish
like Joe.

I asked Dad what you call
someone who is really briliant and
he said 'A jenius. Why?' and I said
'because that is what I'm going to
call my new baby guinea pig' and
he laughed but I said 'You just
wait. One day the World will Know
June 10th is the birthday of
Jenius.'

June 10th was in fact a very good time
for Jenius to have been born, because it
meant that he was around six weeks
old by the time the long summer
holidays began. Now his trainer would
be able to concentrate on him without
the interruption of school.

During those six weeks Jenius had grown amazingly. All baby guinea pigs do, of course, but he had benefited particularly, first from being an only child and so getting all his mother's milk, and secondly from Judy's spoiling.

Ordinary guinea pigs, for example, might get the occasional piece of stale bread. Jenius got regular digestive biscuits.

So that Judy's diary, which had contained daily reports of the progress of the wonder child, read . . .

JULY 22nd: Begining of Summer Hollidays. Today I took Jenius away from his parents and put him in the spare hutch, he is reddy to start his training, he is alreddy half as big as Joe, he is alreddy very good at sitting when he is told because that is what I have consentrated on but now I am going to teach him 'Come' and 'Stay' and 'Down'. Joe and Molly don't seem to miss him.

Joe and Molly were actually quite glad to see the back of Jenius.

Molly was thankful not to be nagged for the milk she no longer had, and Joe, though at first proud of the obvious cleverness of his son, was growing tired of being patronized.

'Thinks he knows it all,' he grumbled to Molly, 'with his "No, Dad, you've got that wrong" or "No, Dad, you don't understand". I said to him: "When you've been around as long as I have, my boy,

then maybe you'll know a thing or two."'

'Quite right, dear,' murmured Molly. 'What did he say then?'

'He said: "When I've been around as long as you have I'll know hundreds of things." Cheeky young devil!'

'Ah well,' sighed Molly. 'He's only young, Joe dear. We're all of us only young once.'

'Molly,' said Joe, 'you're as lovely now as the day I first set eyes on you.'

'Oh, Joe,' said Molly, 'you say the nicest things!'

Chapter Four
A Great Team

'Mum! Mum!' cried Judy, bursting in from the garden with Jenius in her arms. 'Guess what!'

'Not now, Judy,' said her mother. 'I haven't got time for guessing games this morning, what with the washing and the ironing, and I've got a lot of cooking to do, never mind the

housework. Off you run and play, out of my way, please.'

'But, Mum, Jenius comes when he's told!'

'Very clever, dear. Now you go when you're told, there's a good girl.'

'She just didn't listen to what I was saying,' said Judy as she sat on the lawn with Jenius on her lap.

Jenius replied with a small, sympathetic whistle which meant, Judy felt sure, 'Grown-ups are hopeless, aren't they? I expect it'll be just the same when you tell your dad.'

And it was.

'Comes when you call him, does he?' said her father from behind his evening paper.

'Yes, Dad! Honest! Don't you want to see?'

'Not now, pet, I've had a long day. You go and teach your precious genius something else.'

'What like?'

'Oh, reading, writing, some sums. Start with the two-times table – guinea pigs are good at multiplying. Buzz off now, there's a good girl.'

JULY 23rd: I think Mum and Dad grew up in Vicktorian days, they think that childeren should be seen and not herd. I am not going to bother to tell them anything about Jenius any more but only write about him in this dairy so that the World will know how clever he is when I am ~~Ded~~ Dead and Gone.

In the darkness of the garden shed Jenius squeaked from the spare hutch: 'Mum! Dad! Guess what!'

'Not now, dear,' said Molly.

'But guess what I learned today!'

'Hundreds of things, I imagine,' said Joe sourly.

'No, only one. I learned to come when called.'

'Well, now learn to shut up,' said Joe. 'It's late.'

'Your father's right, dear,' said Molly.

'Go to sleep now, there's a good boy.'

Throughout those fine sunny summer holidays the flowering of Jenius came into full bloom.

Judy was the ideal trainer, patient and hard-working, and her new pet was the perfect pupil. He enjoyed his lessons, he learned quickly, and what he had learned he seldom forgot. They made a great team.

AUGUST 15th: Here is a list of the things I have trained Jenius to do:

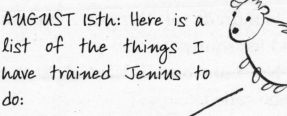

1. COME
2. SIT
3. STAY
4. DOWN
5. WALK ON A LEED

(I do not make him walk to heal because I might tred on him so he walks a little bit in front of me.)

Before the end of the Hollidays I am going to teach him three speshial tricks.

(A) 'Speak'. That is to make a noise when he is told (I suppose I should call this 'SQUEAK').

(B) 'Trust'. That is balancing a bit of biskit on his nose.

(C) 'Die for Your Country.' He has to lie quite still with his eyes shut pretending to be Dead. If I can teach him all these things before the begining of Term I will take him to school and show them all just what a <u>Jenius</u> can do.

Every day trainer and trainee worked at their lessons. And every night Jenius kept his aged parents awake long after their proper bedtime, telling them all

the clever things he had
learned to do. He had
become, it must be said,
a bit of a big-head.

Molly, who was
rather vague by nature,
did not listen very carefully to her
son's boasting, and only
yawned and said
'Very nice, dear,'
now and then, but
Joe became irritable.
'You must be the
most brilliant

guinea pig there
has ever been,' he
would say sourly,
but this did not

improve matters, for Jenius always replied: 'I am, Dad, I am,' in a voice so smug that it made Joe's teeth chatter with rage.

'Cocky young blighter,' he would mutter to Molly. 'One of these fine days he's going to be too clever for his own good.'

And Joe was right. One of those fine days came quite soon.

Chapter Five
Die for Your Country

Jenius had woken early. He looked out of the shed door (which Judy always left open on warm nights) and saw a number of attractive things outside in the garden. There were lettuces and cabbages and the feathery tops of carrots and the shiny dark leaves of beetroot – all very appealing to a growing lad. *Why wait to be fed?* he thought. *I'll feed myself.*

'Mum!' he called. 'I'm going for a walk.'

Molly came to the front of her hutch and looked across the shed.

'Don't be silly, dear,' she said. 'You can't.'

Joe joined her.

'In case you hadn't noticed,' he said sarcastically, 'there's a door on the front of your hutch.'

'Dad,' said Jenius in a patient tone of voice, 'doors are meant to be opened.'

'I know that, boy. By humans. From outside. Not by us from inside. If you can open the door of that hutch from inside, I'll eat my hayrack.'

Each hutch had an outward-opening wire door, kept shut by a five-centimetre turn button, a simple device capable of keeping prisoner every guinea pig that had ever lived. Except the Jenius.

Sitting up on his bottom as he had learned, he reached a forepaw through the wire mesh and turned the button vertically. The door swung open, and down he hopped.

He paused at the entrance to the shed.

'Dad,' he called, 'don't forget to eat your hayrack,' and off he trotted.

What happened next was recorded by a short dramatic entry in the diary.

AUGUST 26th: Jenius got out and was nearly killed! I am keeping the door of the shed shut in case he esscapes again.

Jenius was sitting happily in the sunlit vegetable garden, nibbling a tender young lettuce plant and thinking what

a clever chap he was, when he heard his name called. He looked up and saw Judy leaning out of her bedroom window.

'Whatever are you doing out there?' she said, and since Jenius made no reply, she issued two commands.

'Sit!' she said, and 'Stay!'

Jenius obediently sat down, quite content to remain where he was, in easy reach of such nice food.

Judy was just turning away from her window when, to her horror, she saw the big tabby tom cat from next door drop down from the dividing wall. Slowly, stealthily, he began to stalk the lettuce-eater.

Judy thought frantically. If she left Jenius dutifully sitting and staying, he was a goner. If she called 'Come!' the cat would surely overtake him before she could get downstairs.

There was only one thing to be done, only one order she could give that might perhaps puzzle the hunter for long enough for her to rush to the rescue.

'Jenius!' she yelled in the fiercest, most commanding voice she could manage. 'Die for Your Country!'

CHAPTER SIX
A NIGHTMARE

Jenius, accustomed as he now was to receiving odd orders at odd times, instantly collapsed flat on his back. He stopped chewing his mouthful of lettuce, he closed his eyes, and even the rise and fall of his ribs seemed to have stopped, so lightly did he breathe. He lay, slack and still, looking every inch as he was meant to look. Dead.

'Dead!' said a voice in his ear suddenly.

Jenius's blood ran cold at the sound of this harsh, cruel voice, at the smell of hot, rank breath, at the tickle of long whiskers as something sniffed him all over.

'Pity,' said the cat. 'Could have had a bit of sport if you'd been alive. Ah well, a dead tail-less rat is better than no rat at all,' and with that he began to lick at his victim's head.

Try as he would, Jenius could not keep his upper eye shut. Under the rasp of the cat's tongue the eyelid was pulled back, and he saw, only inches away, a nightmare face. A merciless face it was, with glowing yellow eyes and a wide mouth filled with sharp white teeth.

Despite himself, Jenius gave a little shudder.

'Aha!' hissed the cat. 'Not dead after all!' and he opened that wide mouth. But before he could close it again, a clod of earth hit him on the ear and a furious voice yelled, 'Scat!' as Judy came galloping to the rescue. She

knelt among the lettuce plants beside
the motionless figure of the Jenius.

'It's all right!' she cried. 'He's gone.
You can get up now.'

As always she used the system of
praise-and-reward by which she had
trained him.

'*What* a good boy!' she said, and
from the pocket of her dungarees she
took one of his favourite
digestive biscuits
and broke off
a bit.

Jenius did not
move. Now it was
Judy's blood that
ran cold.

Fearfully she
lifted the limp

body. There was no mark upon it, no blood to be seen.

Could he have died of shock?

'Jenius!' cried Judy frantically in his ear. 'Speak to me. Speak!'

Even though he had fainted with fear at the sheer horror of the experience, the sound of a familiar command was enough to bring him to his senses.

Feebly, through that unchewed mouthful of lettuce, the Jenius obediently uttered a single strangled squeak.

It was a much-reduced Jenius that Judy replaced in his hutch, and when Molly asked: 'Had a nice walk, dear?' he did not answer.

'What's the matter, son?' said Joe. 'Cat got your tongue?'

Chapter Seven
A Bit of a Big-head

AUGUST 26th: Jenius escaped a horribel Death!

Jenius had no intention of escaping again. He had had the fright of his life and, for a little while, his parents were spared their son's bragging and they could enjoy some early nights.

But before long he forgot, and his natural cockiness returned, particularly when he at last mastered the most difficult trick of the exercises that Judy set him. This was the ending to the trick called 'Trust'.

Not only had he to balance a piece of biscuit on the end of his nose, but then, when Judy said, 'Paid for!' he had to toss up the food with a jerk of his head and catch it in his mouth.

Jenius never tired of telling his mother and father how easy this trick was.

'Mind you,' he said, 'I'm the only guinea pig in the world who can do it, I'm sure of that.'

'Very nice, dear,' said Molly absently. 'Pride,' muttered Joe darkly, 'comes before a fall.'

SEPTEMBER 3rd: Jenius has quite recovered. Tomorrow is the last day of the Hollidays and I am going to give him a Test. I am going the to make him do all the things he has been taut and he has got to do them correcktly and I shall give him marks for his performants in each one.

SEPTEMBER 4th: Jenius lived up to his name! He performed perfictly and got Full Marks and I am going to ask my teacher if I can

take him to school and show them
how briliantly I have trained him.
I'm the only person in the world
who could have done it, I'm sure
of that.

Jenius, it must be said, was not the
only one who had become a bit of a
big head, and by the end of the first
day back at school everyone in the
class was fed up with hearing how
clever both he and Judy were. Before
long Judy's teacher too had had
enough.

'Judy,' she said. 'You don't really
expect us to believe all this, do
you?'

'Yes,' said Judy. 'It's true.'

'Well, I'll tell you what. You bring this amazing animal of yours into school and then you can show us all these tricks that you say he can do.'

At once everyone wanted to get in on the act and bring their pet to school.

'Oh, can I bring my rabbit?'

'... my gerbil?'

'... my hamster?'

'... my budgie?'

Until the teacher said: 'All right. We'll have a Pets' Day. You can each bring a pet into school, provided you bring it in a cage or a box – we don't want anything too

big, mind – no Shetland ponies or Great Danes. Who knows, Judy, someone else may have a clever animal too.'

Judy laughed. 'Not as clever as Jenius,' she said scornfully. 'Not possibly. You just wait and see.'

CHAPTER EIGHT
PETS' DAY

Like most people who keep diaries, Judy wrote in hers each evening. But as soon as she woke on the morning that had been chosen for Pets' Day, she opened it.

September 11th: Today it is Pets' Day at school! Jenius will triumph! * Watch this space! *

At breakfast time she could not contain herself. Till now she had said nothing to her parents – as she had sworn on July 23rd – of the progress of the Jenius, but she just knew she would not be able to resist describing the success that was to come before another hour had passed.

'What d'you think is happening today?' she said.

'You're going to be late for school,' said her mother, 'if you don't hurry up. And clean your shoes before you go. And take your anorak – it looks like rain.'

'I'm taking Jenius to school,' said Judy.

'Very nice, dear,' said her mother.

'Now, do you want an apple or a banana in your lunch box?'

'Apple,' said Judy. 'Dad, did you hear what I said?'

'I did,' said her father from behind his morning paper. 'Will he have to start in the Infants or is he clever enough to go straight into your class?'

'Oh, Dad!' cried Judy. 'Honestly, I really have trained him,' and she rattled off a list of the things that Jenius could do.

'Judy,' said her father. 'You don't really expect us to believe all this, do you?'

'Yes,' said Judy. 'It's true.'

Her father folded his newspaper. 'Now look here,' he said. 'Playing pretend games with your precious pet is one thing. But you mustn't confuse fantasy with truth.'

There was hardly room to move in Judy's classroom that morning.

Everywhere there were hutches and cages and baskets and boxes containing pets. Only the Jenius was free, sitting perfectly still in front of Judy.

Judy's teacher saw what seemed to her a rather odd-looking, whitish guinea pig, with a crest of reddish hair sticking up along its back, and said: 'Is this the genius we've heard such a lot about?'

'Yes,' said Judy proudly. 'Shall I show you what he can do?'

Pets

dogs   stic[k]
cats   inse[cts]
mice   rabb[its]
rats   ham[sters]
frogs   snakes
tortoises

'All right,' said her teacher. 'Put him on that big table in the middle of the room where everyone can see him.'

Ranged around the edges of the big table were several pet containers: a couple of hamster cages, a glass jar that held stick insects and a square basket that had one open side barred with metal rods.

Fate decreed that Judy should put the Jenius down quite near to this basket and facing it, and though no one else could see what was in it, he could. He looked through the bars and saw a face, a merciless face, with glowing yellow eyes and a wide mouth filled with sharp white teeth.

In fact the occupant of the basket was only a half-grown kitten, but the sight of it turned Jenius's legs to jelly and scrambled his brains. He was so frightened that he promptly Died for His Country, and there he lay, quite still and barely breathing. He could

hear Judy's voice
saying, 'Come!' and
then, more loudly, 'Jenius! Come!!'
Then he heard a rising tide of noise
which was the whole class first
sniggering, then giggling, and finally
laughing their heads off at clever Judy

and her clever guinea pig, about which she had boasted so loud and long. But he could not move a muscle.

'The great animal trainer!' someone said, and they laughed even more.

'Perhaps that will teach you a lesson, Judy,' said the teacher at last. 'He doesn't seem to be quite the genius you told us he was. You mustn't confuse fantasy with truth.'

CHAPTER NINE
EAT YOUR HAT

'How did you get on, dear, your first day at school?' said Molly that evening.

'Need you ask?' growled Joe. 'You were top of the class, weren't you, son? Got full marks for everything? Performed perfectly, eh?'

'No,' said the Jenius in a small choked voice. 'I didn't do anything.'

'Well, well, well,' said Joe. 'The only guinea pig in the world who can do all those tricks and he didn't do anything. I quite expected you to tell us you did something fantastic ... Hopping like a rabbit perhaps. Or flying like a bird, I shouldn't be surprised.'

Judy came in at that moment with a bunch of dandelions, to hear Joe and Molly making an awful racket. She thought they were yelling for food as usual but actually they were in fits of laughter.

'Flying! Oh, Joe, you are a scream!' squealed Molly, and Joe, snorting with mirth, chuckled, 'Pride comes before a crash-landing!'

A few minutes later Judy's father, home from work, put his head in at the door of the shed.

'Well?' he said. 'And did our genius perform all his amazing tricks?'

'No,' said Judy. 'He wouldn't do anything.'

'Perhaps that will teach you a lesson, Judy,' said her father.

Judy took a deep breath. 'Perhaps it has, Dad,' she said. 'But I wouldn't like you to think I was a liar.'

'It's difficult for me not to think that,' said her father, 'when you tell me such fantastic things. For instance, that your guinea pig can balance something on his nose and then throw

it up and catch it. If he can do that, I'll eat my hat, I promise you.'

'Watch,' said Judy. She took a digestive out of her pocket and broke a

piece off. She opened the
door of Jenius's hutch.

'Come!' she said, and
he came.

'Sit!' she said, and he
sat.

Carefully she placed
the fragment of biscuit on top of Jenius's
snout.

'Trust!' she said, and he remained
sitting bolt upright and stock-still for
perhaps ten seconds, till Judy cried,
'Paid for!'

Up in the air sailed the
bit of digestive and
down it came again,
straight into the
open mouth of the
Jenius.

'*What* a good boy!' said Judy. 'Now you can eat it up.'

She turned to her father, who was bending down, hands on knees, watching in open-mouthed amazement, hat in hand. She took it from him.

'And you,' she said, 'can eat that.'

Funny Frank

Dick King-Smith

Illustrated by John Eastwood

CHAPTER ONE

Jemima Tabb was a farmer's daughter. She was eight years old, she had dark hair worn in a pigtail, and she particularly liked chickens, especially baby chicks.

Whenever one of her father's hens

went broody, Jemima would put a
clutch of eggs under the hen – eggs
that, with luck, would in twenty-one
days' time hatch out into fluffy little
chicks.

Out in the orchard was a duckpond that was fed by a small stream, and not far from the edge of this pond was where Jemima chose to put her broody coop with its wire run attached. *Sitting on eggs must be very boring*, she thought, which is why she selected this spot.

'Just you listen to the chuckle of the water as it falls into the pond, and the sounds of the ducks quacking and splashing about, and you'll find the time will pass quite quickly,' she would say to each broody hen as she settled it upon the eggs.

Three weeks after she had said all this to a hen called Gertie, eight little chicks duly hatched out.

When the chicks first came out of the coop into the wire run, seven of

them scuttled excitedly about on the grass, but the eighth one walked to the end of the run that was nearest to the duckpond and stood there, quite still, listening to the chuckle of the water and the sounds of the ducks quacking and splashing. From then on, he would

do this every day, standing and gazing and listening, so that by the time the chicks were a month old, Gertie – the chicks' mother – was worried and felt she needed to share her worry.

One fine morning when she and her best friend, Mildred, were scratching about together in the orchard, pecking at worms and beetles and the seeds of flowering grasses, Gertie said to Mildred, 'You know, I think that one of my chicks is funny.'

'Funny, Gertie?' clucked Mildred. 'Do you mean funny (ha! ha!) or funny (peculiar)?'

'Peculiar,' replied Gertie. 'I've suspected it for some time now. The other seven chicks behave quite normally but this one's different. To

begin with, he keeps himself to himself.
Look at him now.'

Mildred looked at Gertie's chicks as
they scuttled about in the grass,
pecking at anything and everything,
and she saw that there were only seven

of them doing this. The eighth chick was standing at the edge of the duckpond, looking at the ducks swimming about in it.

'Is that him?' she asked.

'Yes,' replied Gertie.

'Well, he's only looking at the ducks.'

'Yes, I know, Mildred. But *why* is he looking at the ducks?'

'Better ask him,' said Mildred.

'You!' squawked Gertie at the chick. 'Come here!'

At the sound of her voice, the eighth chick turned and came towards them. Usually little chicks run to their mother when she calls them, run very fast, flapping their stubby little wings. But this one was in no hurry.

He came slowly, looking back over his shoulder once or twice at the ducks in the pond, and when he reached the two hens he did not cheep and peep as an ordinary chick would have done. Had Gertie called any one of his brothers and sisters, they would have rushed up to her, saying, 'Yes, Mummy?' and probably adding politely, 'Good morning, Auntie Mildred.'

This chick, though, simply stood there and said, 'What?' He did not

say it in a rude way, but rather in the tone of someone who has been interrupted in the middle of something important.

'Now,' clucked Gertie. 'What were you doing?'

'Looking at the ducks,' her eighth chick replied.

'Yes, but why were you looking at the ducks?'

'I like ducks,' he said. 'They're cleverer than you are, Mum.'

'Cleverer?' squawked Gertie. 'Whatever d'you mean, boy? Compared to hens, ducks are stupid. They can't run about in the grass like we can. They can only waddle.'

'Yes,' said the chick, 'but they can swim. I wish I could. It looks nice.'

'Don't be silly, dear,' his mother said. 'Chickens can't swim. Run along now.'

This time he did run, straight back to the duckpond, and stood once more at the edge.

Gertie shook her head in amazement. 'I told you, Mildred,' she said. 'That chick is funny.'

CHAPTER TWO

Gertie and Mildred moved away down the orchard, shaking their heads in a bewildered fashion. On the pond the ducks dabbled happily, while Gertie's

eighth little chick watched, wishing and wishing that he could dabble too.

What fun it looked to be playing about in all that lovely water that sparkled in the summer sunshine!

How much they were enjoying ducking their heads under, and letting

the glistening stuff slide down their backs, and flapping their wings to spatter themselves with dancing drops, and wagging their rumps with pleasure!

Lucky ducks, he thought. He moved forward a step or two into the shallows at the edge of the pond. How cool the water felt!

Just then a brood of little yellow ducklings came swimming past.

'Excuse me!' the chick called. 'Can I ask you something?'

The fleet of ducklings turned as one, and paddled towards him. 'Ask away, chick,' they cried.

'Well,' he said, 'how did you all learn to swim?'

'Learn?' they cried, and they gave a chorus of shrill squeaks that sounded like laughter.

'We didn't learn,' one said.

'We didn't have to.'

'We just did it.'

'Naturally.'

'Like ducklings do.'

'Well,' said the chick, 'the thing is – I want to learn to swim.'

'Tough luck, chick,' they said.

'Chickens can't swim,' one added.

'Your feathers aren't waterproof.'

'And your feet aren't webbed.'

'So, forget it, chick.'

'But I can't forget it,' said the chick and, in his eagerness to do as the

ducklings did, he took another couple of steps forward till the water was up to his knee joints. 'Don't go!' he called to his new friends. 'Just tell me, what do I do next?'

And with one voice, they called back one word. 'Drown!' And they paddled away making their laughing noises.

The chick took another couple of steps until he felt the water against his breast, and very cold it felt too. At that moment he heard the noise of pounding footsteps, and turned to see Jemima – the farmer's daughter – running

towards him. Then hands grasped
him and scooped him up.

'You silly boy!' said a voice in his
ear. 'Whatever d'you think you're

doing? Anyone would suppose you were trying to swim. Chickens can't, you know. Waterproof feathers and webbed feet – that's what you need for swimming.'

Jemima carried the chick into the kitchen of the farmhouse and was drying his wet bits when her mother came in.

'What have you got there, Jemima?' she asked.

'One of those eight chicks that are out in the orchard, Mum. He was wading into the duckpond, silly boy. Perhaps he thinks he's a duck. I told him, chickens aren't cut out for swimming.'

'And what did he say?'

'He made a funny noise, almost as though he was angry at being picked up.' She held the chick out before her face. 'Didn't you, Frank?'

'Frank? Is that what you are going to call him?' her mother asked.

'Well, that was what the funny noise sounded like. "Frank! Frank!" he squawked. I can't put him back in the orchard, Mum, he'll drown himself, I'm sure he will – won't you, funny Frank?'

'Where are you going to keep him then?'

'I'll put him in that big empty rabbit hutch till I decide what to do. I'll ask Uncle Ted – he might know.'

Uncle Ted was Jemima's father's brother. He was a vet, which was very useful whenever Jemima's father had a sick animal.

Jemima rang her uncle at his surgery.

'Uncle Ted,' she said. 'It's Jemima. I want to ask you about something.

Are you coming anywhere near us today?'

'Yes,' said Ted Tabb, 'as a matter of fact I am. My last call is only a couple of miles from you. I'll look in if you like. About teatime. Just in case your mum has got any of those fruit scones about.'

'Oh, thank you!'

'What's the trouble, Jemima?'

'I've got a chicken that wants to be a duck!'

CHAPTER THREE

'Tea's ready,' called
Jemima's mother. 'Either
of you fancy one of my
fruit scones?' she asked,
just as her husband
and his brother
came into
the
kitchen.

'Yes, please, Carrie,' said Ted, and, 'Me too,' said his brother, Tom, and then, 'What's up then, Ted? I never called you.'

'No, but Jemima did,' said the vet. 'Seems she's got a problem with one of her chicks.'

'I expect you'll sort it out,' said the farmer. 'Mind he doesn't charge you too much, Jemima.'

When a lot of tea had been drunk and the plate of fruit scones was empty, Jemima's father went off to start the afternoon milking.

'Right,' said her uncle. 'Let's have a look at this creature of yours.'

Jemima went outside and took Frank out of the rabbit hutch. 'He's healthy enough, I think, Uncle Ted, isn't he?' she said.

The vet examined the young chicken. 'Looks OK to me,' he said, 'and you're right – by the look of his comb and the set of his tail, he's a cockerel chick.'

'I thought so,' said Jemima. 'I've called him Frank.'

'Well then, Frank,' said Ted, 'let's go down to the duckpond and see what happens.' He went to his car and put on a pair of wellies.

As soon as Frank was put down at the edge of the pond and saw the brood of ducklings come swimming past, squeaking at him, and saw the big ducks dabbling and splashing and preening, and heard them quacking happily to each other, he made up his mind. He would learn to swim. Now! It was now or never. *I'll give it a go*, he said to himself, and he ran straight into the water.

Once out of his depth, he began to flap his little wings wildly, trying to fly (which he couldn't) and kicked madly with his legs, trying to swim (which he couldn't). Already his feathers were soaked, and now he began to sink until only his head was sticking out. From his gaping beak

came one last despairing cry. 'Frank!' he squawked.

'Oh, Uncle Ted, he's going to drown!' cried Jemima just as the little fleet of ducklings sailed by, crying, 'We told you so!'

'No, he isn't,' said her uncle, and he waded out into the pond and picked up the waterlogged bird. 'Looks like you were right, Jemima,' he said. 'Frank does want to be a duck, but he's not exactly equipped for it.'

'No, I know. He needs waterproof feathers and webbed feet.'

'Let's get him dried out,' said the vet, 'and stick him back in the rabbit hutch and I'll have a good think about you, funny Frank. In the meantime, don't let him near that duckpond!'

The very next day Jemima's Uncle Ted turned up at the farm again. 'I've had an idea,' he said. 'About Frank.'

'What is it?' Jemima asked.

'Well, there can only be one reason for him going into the duckpond, and that is that he wants to swim. Now then, suppose we could help him to do that, make it safe for him to go in the water. He'd be as happy as a pig in muck, Frank would, paddling around with the ducks, wouldn't he now.'

'Oh yes!' said Jemima. 'But how? I mean, his feathers . . . his feet . . .'

'Tell me this, Jemima,' said Ted Tabb. 'When people go surfing at the seaside, no matter how cold the sea is, what do they wear?'

'Wetsuits, you mean?' said Jemima.

'Yes,' said her uncle. 'Go and ask your mum if she's got an old hot-water bottle she could spare . . .'

Chapter Four

Frank's mother, Gertie, was extremely worried. She was a very conventional hen who, in her time, had hatched a great many broods of chicks, all of whom had – she liked to think – been properly brought up. That is to say, they were well-mannered and did as they were told and behaved in every way as chicks should.

Now she had somehow managed to produce this funny son, Frank, who was acting in such a very odd fashion. She had seen him with her own eyes walk into the duckpond right up to his knees before the girl had come running to save him.

'Let's hope that will teach him a lesson,' she had said to her friend Mildred. 'I don't think he'll do that again in a hurry.'

But she had been wrong. He had done it again, the same day, and Mildred had seen him do it.

Mildred was by nature a pokenose who liked to stick her beak into everyone else's business. She was also a gossip and she had made sure that the rest of the flock had heard the news before she ran to the bottom of the orchard to tell Gertie about Frank's latest exploit.

'You'll never guess what's happened to Frank!' she panted. 'Oh dear, oh dear, it's the end! *Poor Gertie*, I thought. There was just his little head sticking out of the water, and him calling for help, oh dear, oh dear!'

'He's drowned!' screeched Gertie. 'My little Frank, he's drowned!'

'I don't think so, dear,' said Mildred. 'The girl was there with a man who waded into the pond, rescued your little lad and took him away. But oh my, what a worry it must be for you, having a son like that.'

'Like what?' said Gertie.

'Well,' said Mildred, 'sort of, you know, not quite . . .'

'Not quite what?' said Gertie rather sharply.

'Well, not quite, er, right in the head,' replied Mildred with an embarrassed cackle.

'Mildred,' said Gertie slowly and deliberately, 'we have been friends for many years, you and I. After your last remark, we are friends no longer.' And she stalked off.

*

The next morning Gertie was sitting in one of the nest boxes in the henhouse when Mildred appeared.

'Good morning, Gertie dear,' she said.

'It is *not* a good morning,' replied Gertie, 'and I am about to lay an egg. Kindly go away.'

'But I have something important to tell you, dear,' said Mildred.

'And I have something important to do, Mildred. Something private and personal. A well-bred hen expects some privacy when she is sitting in her nest box, for a purpose. I don't wish to do it with someone looking on.'

'Oh, sorry, dear,' said Mildred. 'I'll tell you later on.' And she went away.

As soon as she was gone, Gertie raised herself a little and, with a slightly strained expression on her face, laid an egg. She stood up and turned to inspect it. It was, she saw with satisfaction, of a good size and a good colour – a handsome shade of brown. Gertie, something of a snob, rather despised hens that laid white eggs.

Now she stepped from the nest box, gave that shout of triumph that all hens make after laying and made her way out of the henhouse. Mildred was waiting by the pop-hole.

'Well?' said Gertie.

'What is this important thing you wish to tell me?'

'It's about Frank, Gertie,' said Mildred. 'I was having a little look around the place and happened to see him.'

'Where?'

'In a rabbit hutch.'

Oh no! thought Gertie. *First he wants to be a duck. Now he wants to be a rabbit.* 'A rabbit hutch!' she said. 'Poor boy! No room to move about.'

'No,' said Mildred, 'but at least you can't drown in a rabbit hutch!'

Chapter Five

Jemima's mother did have an old hot-water bottle that no one ever used.

'But why d'you want it?' she asked Jemima.

'Uncle Ted wants it.'

'Whatever for?'

313

Just then the vet came in.

'Whatever do you want a hot-water bottle for, Ted?' asked his sister-in-law. 'Is it to keep a lamb warm?'

'No, Carrie,' said Ted Tabb. 'It's to keep a chicken dry. Can I borrow your tape measure? We must make it fit properly.'

'Make what fit?'

'A wetsuit, Mum,' said Jemima. 'For Frank. So that he can swim.'

'Actually we'd be glad of your help, Carrie,' said the vet. 'I know you're a good dressmaker.'

'You're crazy, the pair of you,' Jemima's mother said. But to herself she said, *If it's worth doing, it's worth doing well.*

First they took Frank out of the rabbit hutch and made careful notes of his measurements – the length of his back, the breadth of his breast – then they held the hot-water bottle up against him to try for size.

With her dressmaking shears, Jemima's mother cut off the mouth of the bottle and cut right round the edges of it to make two rubber panels. 'One

for his front, one for his back,' she said, 'and then I'll stick them together.'

'Remembering,' said Ted, 'to leave a hole at the end for his head and neck to stick out. Oh yes, and two holes for his legs and another for his tail.'

'What about his wings?' Jemima asked.

'Oh yes, and two holes for his wings. He can use those to pull himself along through the water, like an oarsman. It won't matter if they get wet.'

'Well, I can't guarantee,' said Jemima's mother, 'that the finished article will be completely waterproof of course, but it should keep most of him pretty dry.'

Between the three of them they managed to hold a protesting Frank and place the two rubber panels against him – front and back – testing for size.

'It'll be miles too big,' Jemima said.

'It will now,' said her mother, 'but don't forget Frank's going to grow. And I'm not making him a whole lot of different-sized wetsuits. This one will have to do.'

'Let me know how you get on,' said the vet. 'I must be off.'

Carrie Tabb had never before set out to make a wetsuit for a chicken, but before long Frank was having his first fitting so that she could see exactly where to make the holes for neck, wings, legs and tail. This done, the two panels of the old hot-water bottle were put on Frank, front and back, and then the two halves were stuck together with superglue.

At first Frank protested loudly at the treatment he was receiving, but once the finished wetsuit was finally fitted on him, he seemed to be quite pleased with himself and walked about and flapped his wings and shouted, 'Frank!' in a loud voice.

That evening, when Tom Tabb had finished milking his cows, he rang up his brother, the vet.

'What time will you finish your surgery, Ted?' he asked.

'About seven, I hope.'

'Well, come on over then. Carrie has made this suit for Jemima's chicken and they're going to try it out.'

'On the duckpond?'

'Yes. Seeing as it was your crazy idea, you'd better come to the ceremony. You're invited to the launch of Frank.'

So, later, the four Tabbs stood at the edge of the duckpond, wetsuited Frank in Jemima's arms. Around the pond Frank's brothers and sisters were standing, and Gertie and Mildred, and all the other hens of the flock, and the big cockerel. They knew what was going to happen because gossipy Mildred had told them. On the water the ducks and their ducklings cruised.

Now Jemima, in her wellies, waded out into deeper water and carefully

lowered Frank on to the surface and let go of him.

He floated.

Loudly the ducks on the pond quacked in amusement. A chicken that floated – weird!

Around the rim the hens squawked in amazement, and the big cockerel gave a loud crow of surprise while

Frank's brothers and sisters scampered up and down in excitement.

'He's swimming!' gasped Gertie to Mildred as she gazed upon her wetsuited son.

'Well, not exactly, dear,' replied Mildred. 'He's floating, certainly, but he's not going anywhere much. He'd have to have webbed feet for that.'

Frank was indeed trying to swim. He bashed on the water with his wings and he kicked about with his legs, but neither method propelled him very far. It was plain that Mildred was right, and the watching Tabbs came to the same conclusion.

'You said he'd pull himself along with his wings like an oarsman,' said Jemima to her uncle, 'but he can hardly move.'

'He's too heavy with all that gear on,' said her father, and then farmer and vet said with one voice, 'He needs webbed feet.'

'Right,' said Jemima's mother. 'Then it's back to the drawing board!'

Chapter Six

'We can't just leave him there, floating about,' said Jemima.

'Go and get some corn and feed the rest of the flock,' said her father.

'Yes,' said her uncle. 'Frank will come out of the pond quick enough then.'

And indeed, once Jemima had scattered some handfuls of corn in the orchard grass and the rest were all pecking away at it, Frank managed slowly to scull his way to the pond's edge until at last his feet touched bottom and he could, very clumsily, run to join the others.

All this time, Jemima had been watching, and now she saw that all the corn had been eaten, leaving none for Frank. So she fetched another handful just for him and kept the rest away while he ate, scratching at the little heap of corn with his long toes. *Great for scratching*, thought Jemima, *great for running on the grass, but useless for swimming.* How could they help him?

She watched as Frank pecked up the last grain of corn and then looked up at her enquiringly, head on one side.

'You're a bright boy, Frank, aren't you?' she said. 'You look at me as though you can understand what I'm

saying. I just wish you weren't such a worry to us, wanting to swim like a duck. I suppose you're going to go straight back on the pond now?'

For answer, Frank did. He walked right in till he was out of his depth, and then he floated out towards the ducks.

The ducklings were the first to greet him.

'Hi there, chick!' they cried. 'That's a cool suit you're wearing!'

'Actually,' said Frank, 'it's rather hot in the sunshine, when I'm on land, I mean.'

'*East, west, water's best,*' chorused the ducklings and away they swam.

Frank worked his legs madly in an effort to follow his young friends, but

his clawed
feet
simply
could
n o t
propel
him
along,
a n d
fluttering his wings was little help and very tiring. *If only I had feet like a duck,* he thought, *so that I could thrust with my feet like they do and push the water away behind me and go sailing along instead of just floating. If only those humans would realize that that's what I need. They were clever enough to make me this wetsuit. Surely they could think of some way to make me webs?*

Jemima's mother, Carrie, *had* been thinking. How could she design a pair of artificial webbed feet? She racked her brains for some way to do this, and then, by sheer chance, the answer came to her as she was cleaning the bathroom later that evening. She was wearing a pair of rubber gloves as she filled the wash basin and scoured it around. They were bright yellow, these gloves, and some combination of thoughts about yellow gloves and ducks' feet and water gave her the idea. She could – she would – make a pair of artificial webbed feet out of the rubber gloves. *I'll put something inside the fingers and thumbs to stiffen them,* she said to herself, *to help Frank walk (or waddle, rather) on dry land. Then I'll get a*

sheet of something solid – plywood, perhaps; no, plastic, that'll be lighter – and I'll cut out two pieces the shape of a duck's foot and fix one inside each glove like a sort of inner sole. Then all we shall have to do is *stick Frank's feet inside and tape the cuff of each glove around his legs so that no water can get in and, hey presto! Frank will have webbed feet!*

CHAPTER SEVEN

One of Jemima's jobs about the farm
was, in the evening, to shut up the
hens and the ducks in their respective
houses, to keep them safe from foxes.
She left her mother working on the
artificial webbed feet and went out
into the orchard.

Sleepy murmurs from the henhouse
told her that the flock had already gone

to bed, and automatically she bent to close the pop-hole when she thought, *Oh, Frank! Is he inside?* She opened the door of the henhouse. He wasn't.

She went to the duckhouse, outside which several ducks and the big white drake were still pottering about, preening and gabbling softly to one another.

Jemima hooshed them into the house and looked inside, to see all the ducks and all the ducklings – but no Frank.

Quickly she shut the duckhouse door and ran to the duckpond. There, still floating happily out in the middle, was Frank.

When the ducks had begun to leave the pond and waddle away towards the duckhouse, Frank had been in no hurry to follow. He had become rather hot, wearing as he was a rubber suit

over his plumage, and now floating on the nice cold water as the heat went out of the day and the sun sank was so refreshing.

'You coming, chick?' the ducklings called out as they swam past following their mother.

'It's time for beddy-byes.'

'I think I'll stay here for a bit,' Frank replied. 'I'm enjoying it.'

'Please yourself,' they said. 'Let's just hope that someone else doesn't enjoy you.'

'Who?' asked Frank.

'Mr Fox!' cried the ducklings, and they scuttered off.

For a while Frank continued to float about on the pond, trying to decide what to do. *Surely I'll be safe out in the middle here*, he thought. *Foxes can't*

swim. Can they? Just then he heard his name called.

'Frank!' cried Jemima. 'Come off the pond, you silly boy.'

When he made no move, she found a long stick and waded in till the water was near the tops of her wellies and

reached out and managed to hook Frank with the stick and pull him to shore. Jemima picked him up and carried him to the henhouse, but when she went to open the door, he kicked and struggled and squawked and shouted, 'Frank!' in an angry voice.

So she took him to the duckhouse. As soon as she opened its door, he jumped out of her arms and rushed in.

When she had closed the door, Jemima listened for a moment. Inside, the ducks were gabbling quietly and the ducklings peep-peeping – in a show of welcome, she thought.

In reply her young cockerel said his name several times.

Strange, Jemima thought. *It's beginning to sound more like 'Quack!' than 'Frank!'*

'What d'you think of these then, Tom?' said Carrie Tabb to her husband, holding out the results of her handiwork.

The farmer picked one up and inspected it. 'By golly, that's a duck's foot and a half,' he said. 'Grand pair of flippers they'll make.'

'More like galoshes really,' said Jemima's mother. 'Don't forget that Frank has to be able to walk in them as well as swim in them.'

'When are you going to fit them on him?'

'Tomorrow morning. Jemima can catch Frank when she lets the hens out.'

'No, she can't,' said Jemima, coming in. 'He wouldn't go to bed with the

hens, he's in the duckhouse. Anyway, why must I catch him?'

Her mother and father pointed – one with pride, one with amusement – at the strange pair of artificial webbed feet, bright yellow with five stiffened claws (that had been four

fingers and a thumb) and, inside each rubber glove, a piece of stout plastic cut to the shape of a duck's foot.

'Oh, Mum, you are clever!' Jemima said. 'I can't wait to see if they work properly.'

'Well, wait till I've finished tomorrow morning's milking,' said her father. 'This is something I don't want to miss.'

When, next day, the farmer came into the orchard, his wife and daughter were ready and waiting. They had fitted the new feet to Frank and taped the cuffs of the gloves securely around each leg. He looked a picture, with his brown head and wings and tail poking out of his green hot-water-bottle wetsuit and his yellow rubber-glove webs.

Jemima put the young cockerel down on the grass. For a moment Frank stood still, puzzled by the strange things that had been put on his feet. Then he began to walk, lifting each foot high and then putting it down again flat on the ground, rather like a man in snowshoes. He tripped himself up once or twice due to the

size of his new webs, but then he got more used to them and began to make his way towards the duckpond. He sploshed in the shallows and walked on in till he was floating.

Jemima held her mother's hand tightly. 'Oh, Mum, it will work, won't it?' she said.

'Fingers crossed,' said her mother, and they all three crossed them.

Then, as they watched, Frank began to make strong thrusts with his long legs, just the movements he would have made to run on dry land, and immediately he began to move forward, slowly at first, then faster, faster, till he was swimming around the pond at a speed no duck could hope to match. All the other ducks in fact got hastily

out of the way lest they be rammed by
this speeding water bird.

'Wow!' the ducklings cried as he
whizzed by. 'What a swimmer!'

Farmer Tabb summed up the general
amazement. 'Cor lumme, luvaduck!'
he said.

Chapter Eight

Gertie and Mildred had gone back into the henhouse to lay their day's eggs, and so knew nothing of Frank in all his finery.

They were sitting in adjoining nest boxes,

and Mildred – mindful of the rebuke she had recently received for speaking while Gertie was laying – kept her beak shut.

Once Mildred had performed and gone out, Gertie laid her egg and then had a look at Mildred's in the next box. It was, she was pleased to see, a white egg of rather a poor size. *Badly bred, Mildred is*, she said to herself with satisfaction. *I always knew it.* Suddenly,

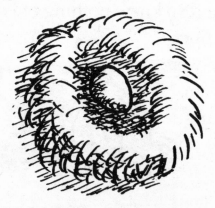

outside, she saw Mildred scuttling back at speed.

'Quickly, dear,' Mildred panted. 'Come and have a look at your Frank!'

'I want nothing more to do with the boy,' said Gertie. 'He's nothing but an embarrassment to me.'

'But you must come and look,' said Mildred. 'He's really swimming!'

Curiosity is a strong instinct, and Gertie could not resist making her way to the duckpond. At the furthest side of it, she saw, was her son, sitting upon the water, quite still.

'If you call that swimming, my dear Mildred,' said Gertie in a very sarcastic voice, 'you need your brains examining – if you've got any. Frank is simply floating as he has done before, thanks to that awful rubber suit.'

Frank was in fact getting his breath back after a great number of high-speed circuits of the pond, but when he saw his mother on the opposite side, he shouted, 'Mum! Watch this!' and set off towards her as fast as his webs could drive him. Which was very fast. Up out of the water he

surged and stood proudly before his mother in his wetsuit and new yellow footwear.

'What d'you think, Mum?' he said.

For answer, Gertie gave a loud squawk of horror and ran hastily away. What had her son done now! Mildred ran away too, eager to tell the rest of the flock about this latest development.

Frank turned sadly back towards the pond. Over its surface there still ran the waves caused by his recent rapid dash, and on them the ducklings bobbed.

'Wow!' they cried. 'You're the greatest!'

'Greatest what?' asked Frank.

'Why, swimmer, of course,' they said. 'Fan-tastic!'

Frank felt a glow of warmth. His mother didn't want to have anything to do with him, nor did his brothers

 and
sisters,
nor the
big
cockerel,
nor any of the
hens in the flock. But these little
ducklings – they were his friends.

'I really *can* swim now, can't I?' he
said.

'And how!' cried the ducklings.

'Can I come for a swim with you all
now?' Frank asked.

The ducklings looked at each other.

'OK,' one said.

'On one condition,' said another.

'What?' said Frank.

'Take it a bit slow, chick.'

'There's no hurry.'

'Nice and easy does it.'

'You may like the high-speed stuff . . .'

'. . . but we don't.'

'Oh, I see what you mean,' Frank said. 'If I'm dashing about, it makes the water rough so it's not so nice for you. Is that it?'

'You got it,' they all said. 'It's enough to make us pondsick.'

So Frank launched himself back into the water very carefully, and began to swim gently around the duckpond with slow measured thrusts of his big yellow webbed feet and the little yellow ducklings swam with him, like a flotilla of small boats escorting a big ship.

Then the big white drake and all the other ducks, seeing how the ducklings

were enjoying the company of the strange chicken, came out on to the water and swam along too, so that Frank found himself at the head of a great armada of ducks.

At last, he thought happily, *I am in my element!*

CHAPTER NINE

It so happened that later that day one of Tom Tabb's best cows was having difficulty in calving and so he sent for his brother the vet.

Later, when the calf had been safely delivered – a heifer calf at that, which pleased the farmer – Ted Tabb asked how Jemima's Frank was getting on.

'You'll be amazed,' Tom said. 'Carrie has made him artificial feet. I'll just go and get a bowl of corn and we'll go down to the duckpond and you'll see.'

By chance all the ducks and the ducklings too were pottering about in the orchard grass, so that the pond was empty of birds except for Frank.

He had been trying to copy his friends, who were so good at putting their heads below the surface to pull up weeds or snap up wiggly things. *If I'm going to be a proper duck*, he told himself, *I've got to be able to do that*, and so he had been practising. But somehow he didn't seem to have the knack of it. He could put his head under all right (though not very far – the wetsuit would not allow it), but he wasn't too clever at holding his breath or keeping

his beak closed so that the water got up his nostrils and down his throat. Altogether he was fed up and glad to see the two men approaching, one holding a bowl of corn and calling him by name.

Frank went into overdrive. He whizzed across the surface of the pond so fast that he shot out of the water on to the bank, landing flat-footed on his big yellow webs.

'What d'you think of that?' asked the farmer.

'Amazing!' said the vet. 'Look at those feet! What a rate he goes! Carrie's a genius. But, Tom, what's to become of this funny bird that is a chicken but wants to be a duck?'

'Blessed if I know, Ted,' said his brother. 'I hope he doesn't come to any harm, Jemima's that proud of him. We'll just have to wait and see.'

So they waited, as the weeks and indeed the months went by, and they saw Frank grow and grow till he was almost the size of his father, the big red rooster. (Or rather, as big as his father had *been*, for one day, down at the far end of the orchard, he had met an old dog fox that had hidden itself in

a nettle patch.) On Frank's head now was a big floppy scarlet comb, while out of the back of the wetsuit there hung a fine plumy tail. His wings too had grown enormously so that now he could really scull with them to make his speedy progress on water even speedier.

All this time Frank spent his nights in the duckhouse and his days on the duckpond, only coming ashore for food. Of his mother he saw practically nothing, for she kept well away from him, as indeed did his brothers and sisters and the rest of the flock. Sometimes this made Frank feel a little sad, for he was after all a chicken at heart. He had his friends, the ducks, but the older he got the more he began to realize that though he could swim like a duck – far better, in fact – he could never look like one.

He would see his three brothers come strutting by and think how handsome they had grown with their fine feathers and their elegant sharp-clawed feet, in contrast to his clumsy green rubber suit and his awkward yellow rubber webs.

A little later he noticed that there were only two of his brothers, and later still only one, and at last none. Where had they gone? Frank wondered. Little did he dream that they had made three plump Sunday dinners for the Tabb family.

For a long time Frank had tried hard, too, to copy the sounds that all the ducks made – his first friends, the ducklings, were grown up now – but

his 'Quack!' was really still only
'Frank!' But then, one fine morning,
something quite unexpected happened
to funny Frank . . .

Jemima had let the hens out, and
then had opened the duckhouse door,

and all the ducks and the big white drake and Frank came out and made for the pond as usual.

The waterfowl went straight on to the water but Frank, instead of following, jumped clumsily up on top of a big log that lay by the pond's edge. He stood up on his toes (as best he could on his artificial feet, which was not very well), puffed out his chest (though this action, within the wetsuit, could not be seen), stretched out his (by now, very long) neck and, to the astonishment of the ducks, gave a loud, piercing 'Cock-a-doodle-doo!'

Chapter Ten

'He crowed, did he?'
said Jemima's father
when she told him.

'Yes,' said
Jemima. 'That
means he's a
proper grown-
up cockerel now,
doesn't it, Dad?'

The farmer looked thoughtful. 'You know, Jemima,' he said, 'I think it's time you thought this business through – I mean, about Frank wanting to be a duck. OK, he enjoys swimming in the pond, but it's not natural. He should be running around with the rest of the flock, stretching his legs, preening his feathers, behaving like the chicken he is. He can't do any of that while he's dressed up in bits of an old hot-water bottle and a pair of rubber gloves.'

'Well, what d'you think I should do, Dad?' asked Jemima.

'Nothing for the present. But I think we've got to give him something to tempt him out, something that will be more attractive to him than the ducks.'

'Like what?'

'Well,' said Jemima's father, 'now that he's a big boy, what he needs is a nice girlfriend. That'd really give him something to crow about. Tell you what, next market day, I'll have a look around the poultry pens and see if I can find a pretty little pullet for your Frank.'

Frank, too, was thinking of his future. As he watched the flock running helter-skelter across the orchard when Jemima came with food, as he saw them scratching about in the grass or taking a dust bath and then preening their feathers, he began increasingly to feel that he had become a prisoner of his own ambition. Because he had wanted to swim like a duck, was he to spend the rest of his life stuck inside his wetsuit so that he couldn't preen or have a dust bath, with his feet confined in his artificial webs so that he couldn't scratch and couldn't run? He remembered how his late father, the big red rooster, had strutted noisily and proudly among his many brown wives. Was he, Frank, never to have a wife of his own?

Over the next couple of days he found himself spending less time on the water and more on the land. At feeding times, he even tried talking to some of the flock, and went as far as saying, 'Hello, Mum, how are you?' to Gertie, but she did not answer.

Jemima, meanwhile, was consulting her mother. She it was, after all, who had been to all the trouble of designing Frank's swimming costume.

'What d'you think, Mum?' she said. 'Should we take it off him? He doesn't seem to want to swim as much as he used to.'

'If we take it off him, he won't be able to, will he?'

'Can't we just try and see what happens?'

'OK, we'll do it tomorrow. I'm a bit busy today.'

As things turned out, it was just as well that Jemima's mum postponed the undressing of Frank. For that evening, the old dog fox sneaked back and lay up once more in the nettle patch. Most of the flock had already made their way up to the henhouse and only Gertie and Mildred were still down at the far end of the orchard, having a last forage in the grass.

Though they were not as firm friends as they had once been, Mildred had partly wormed her way back into Gertie's good books, mostly by toadying to her. Now, looking up at the sky, she said, 'Don't you think it's getting late, dear? Time for bed. Come along now.'

Gertie did not like to be told. 'I'll come when I'm good and ready,' she said.

Frank was still standing by the edge of the duckpond. The ducks had gone in, but he stayed, his eye on his distant mother. *I'll try and have a word with her as she goes by,* he thought. *She might give me some advice on what to do.*

As he peered down the darkening orchard, he saw the figure of Mildred approaching.

'Isn't Mum coming?' he asked her.

'Don't know, I'm sure,' said Mildred huffily as she went by.

I'd better go down and see what she's doing, thought Frank. *It'll be dark soon.* But then he saw his mother turn and begin to walk up the orchard towards him.

Then he saw a bushy-tailed red shape emerge from the nettle patch and follow . . .

Chapter Eleven

'Mum!' yelled Frank at the top of his voice. 'Behind you! Look behind you!' and Gertie, doing as she was told for once, came scuttling towards him, wings flapping madly, squawking in panic.

Chickens have always run away from foxes, and Frank should now have fled too. For a moment he was paralysed with fear, knowing that he'd

be too slow to escape. But then, unable
to bear the sight of his terror-stricken
old mother, he set off bravely straight
towards the oncoming fox.

'Keep going, Mum!' he cried as
Gertie dashed past, and then he
marched on towards the old enemy,
lifting his great yellow webs high and
stamping them down again while
loudly crying, 'Frank! Frank!'

The fox stopped in his tracks. What kind of chicken was this that was coming directly at him, shouting some kind of war cry? What kind of chicken was this that wore

a coat of green armour, that had huge webbed feet, and smelled strongly of duckpond? The old dog fox's nerve broke, and he turned tail and slunk away.

Just then, Jemima came out into the orchard to shut the ducks and chickens up for the night. She heard her cockerel's cries and ran, just in time to see the worsting of the fox. 'Oh, Frank, Frank!' she called, and then she hurried to pick him up.

'What a brave boy you are!' she said as she carried him to the duckhouse.

But when she came to its door, he kicked and struggled and squawked and shouted his name in an angry voice. So she took him to the henhouse, and he jumped out of her arms and dashed in.

On one of the perches, a breathless Gertie had been telling Mildred what had happened.

'There was a fox . . .' she panted.

'I told you, didn't I?' said Mildred. 'I told you it was getting late.'

'Oh, be quiet and listen,' said Gertie, 'because if it hadn't been for Frank, you would never have heard my voice again.'

'Oh dear, oh dear,' said Mildred.

'He saved my life!' said Gertie. 'He charged at that fox so that I could have time to escape. I only hope he died quickly. Oh, my brave Frank, he gave his life for mine.' She closed her eyes and sat in silent mourning.

'I don't think he did, dear,' said Mildred, for at that moment Frank came dashing in through the henhouse door, which Jemima closed behind him.

Gertie opened her eyes to see, standing in the gloom, the rubber-clad figure of her son. 'It's a ghost!' she murmured to Mildred in horror.

'I don't think it is, dear,' said Mildred.

'I'm not a ghost, Mum,' said Frank. 'I'm solid flesh and blood.'

'And rubber,' said Mildred.

'Yes, I think that's what scared that old fox. He'd never seen a cockerel like me.'

'There's never *been* a cockerel like you, my boy!' cried Gertie. 'You saved Mummy's life! You're a hero!'

Frank looked down his beak modestly.

'And it's lovely to have you back here with us instead of being with those old ducks,' said Gertie. *I daresay it was his funny gear that frightened that fox,* she thought drowsily as she drifted towards sleep. *But I wish he'd get rid of it . . .*

Chapter Twelve

The very next day Jemima's father went to market and found just what he'd been looking for.

'Come and see what I've got for you,' he said to his daughter when he arrived home. He took a crate out of the back of the Land Rover.

'Oh, Dad!' cried Jemima. 'Is it a girlfriend for Frank?'

'Yes. What d'you think of her?'

Jemima lifted out of the crate a pullet of a particularly pretty colour. She was not brown like all the other hens in the flock. She was speckled, her white feathers covered in little black dots.

'She's gorgeous!' cried Jemima softly. 'Shall I take her out and introduce her to Frank?'

'I think I'd leave it till the morning,' said Tom Tabb. 'It's getting late; it'll be dark soon. Stick her in the old rabbit hutch for tonight with some food and water and we'll put her out tomorrow.'

'Tomorrow,' Jemima said, 'Mum's going to take Frank's wetsuit and webs off.'

'Wait till she has, then. This little girl might get a bit of a shock if she meets Frank in all his funny gear.'

She won't get a shock, thought Jemima as she lay in bed that night. *She'll probably think he looks really cool.*

So next morning, when she went to let the flock out, she caught up Frank

and carried him to the rabbit hutch.
Frank looked in, to see a vision of
speckled beauty. He let out a strangled
croak. It was love at first sight!

The pullet's reaction at seeing him
was rather different. She put her head
on one side and regarded him with a
bright eye.

'Coo-er!' she said. 'You don't half
look funny.'

'Funny (ha! ha!) or funny (peculiar)?' asked Frank.

'Both,' replied the pullet and she turned her back on him.

Frank looked crestfallen.

'Don't worry,' Jemima said to him. 'Wait till we get all that old stuff off you.'

With the help of her mother, she unstuck the wetsuit and took off the artificial webs, then Jemima took Frank out into the orchard and let him go.

Hope he doesn't try to swim now, she thought, ready to rescue him if he should. But grown-up Frank seemed to have more sense. To be sure, he waded a little way into the pond on his long legs to say good morning to his web-footed friends, but no further. Then he ran lightly off and began to scratch about in the grass with those sharp claws he'd never properly used,

and gave himself a good dust bath, and shook his bright-red feathers, hidden for so long under their rubber covering, and began thoroughly to preen himself. Then he jumped easily on to the top of the big log and stood up on his toes and puffed out his chest and stretched out his neck and crowed a loud, triumphant crow.

Gertie had just re-entered the henhouse to lay an egg when Mildred came dashing in.

'Quickly, come quickly, dear!' she screeched.

'I have told you before, Mildred –' began Gertie, but Mildred continued, unabashed.

'It's Frank!' she cried. 'You'll never guess!' and she rushed out again.

Frank, from having been the bane of Gertie's life, was now – thanks to his saving of that life – the apple of her eye, and she forgot both her cry of triumph at laying and her dignity and went tearing after her friend.

'Where is he? What's happened? Is he all right?' she cried, and then she saw, standing upon the log by the pond, a magnificent young red cockerel. *Who's he?* she thought. 'Where's my Frank?' she said.

'There, dear,' said Mildred. 'On the log. That's him. They've taken his clothes off. Isn't

he handsome!' And as she spoke,
Frank gave another loud, triumphant
crow.

At that moment Jemima came out
carrying the speckled pullet and put
her down on the grass and watched
her scamper towards the new Frank
and stop by the log to gaze up at him.

'Hello,' said the pullet. 'Where have
you been all my life?'

Inside a wetsuit, thought Frank. 'I think we've met before,' he gulped.

'We certainly have not,' replied the speckled pullet. 'The only guy I've met since I arrived last evening was a weird-looking wally dressed up as a duck. As different from you as could be. Hope I don't meet him again.'

'You won't,' said Frank. 'He's gone. By the way, my name's Frank. What's yours?'

'Haven't really got a name,' she said. 'My mum just called us all "chick".'

Frank hopped off the log and stood beside her. 'I'd call you gorgeous,' he murmured softly.

'I like it!' cried the speckled pullet. 'Sounds nice. You're Frank, I'm Gorgeous.'

'Oh, my!' said Mildred from where she and Gertie were standing. 'How I should love to know what they're saying!'

Normally Gertie would have replied to such a remark with a cutting answer such as 'The world would be a better place if everybody minded their own business.' But now she stood in a kind of daze, staring at her handsome hero of a son and the new arrival. *She looks*

to be well-bred, she thought, *and that speckled colour is so distinguished. I bet she will lay the brownest of eggs.* Then she saw the pullet run off down the orchard, pursued by her boy.

'Don't they make a lovely couple, dear!' said Mildred. 'You'll be having more pretty grandchildren one of these fine days.'

'Mildred,' said Gertie dreamily. 'For once, you're right.'

The rest of the flock had been staring too, first at the new-look Frank and then at the very pretty pullet. The ducks, too, watched proceedings with much interested quacking.

'We miss Frank,' those ducks that had once been his little duckling friends said to their father, the big white drake. 'D'you think he'll ever come swimming with us again, Dad?'

'He will not,' said the drake. 'He's a nice boy, Frank is, but it wasn't wise of him to try and be a duck. Ducks are cleverer than chickens, you see. We can walk about *and* we can swim. Chickens can only walk about. They can't swim.'

That afternoon Carrie Tabb tempted her brother-in-law, the vet, to come over to tea (she'd just made a fresh batch of fruit scones), and so the four of them – Tom and Carrie, Jemima and her Uncle Ted – leaned on the orchard gate and watched as Frank strutted proudly past, Gorgeous at his side.

'Funny, Frank, wasn't he?' said Jemima.

'How d'you mean?' they said.

'Well, wanting so much to be a duck. He doesn't any more, does he?'

'He's found his true place,' they said.

'And his true love!' said Jemima, and they all smiled happily.

Frank and Gorgeous stood wing tip to wing tip by the edge of the duckpond. Frank's friends swam by, loudly quacking his name in greeting.

'Stupid creatures!' said Gorgeous, tossing her pretty head. 'Sploshing about in that stuff. Why, water's only for drinking, any fool knows that.'

'I suppose so,' said Frank, 'but don't you ever think it would be nice to be able to swim?'

'To swim?' cried Gorgeous. 'A chicken, swimming? Oh, Frank, you are funny!'

Dick and Dodo's Book of Pets

Dick King-Smith

Illustrated by Ann Kronheimer

When I was small I had a favourite book. I've still got it, though a lot of the pages are loose or dog-eared or even torn because it's so old. It was written long before I was born, and it's called *Pets and How to Keep Them*.

It seems very old-fashioned now, but I still feel that the man who wrote it had thought a lot about what the word 'pet' means.

Have you?

If you look it up in the dictionary it says: 'Pet – a cherished tame animal', and then you look up 'cherished' and it means somebody or something that's taken care of and treated with affection. So that's what a pet is – an animal you look after and love.

Dodo is a miniature wire-haired dachshund and is one of my wonderful pets.

Dodo and I are going to look at lots of different animals that make good pets. Maybe you already have one of them. Maybe you've always wanted one, but haven't been lucky yet. But whatever your pet is, whether it's a valuable dog like Dodo or a tiddly little goldfish you won at a fair, be sure to cherish it.

Dodo

Most people in the UK are fond of all sorts of dogs, whether they are huge wolfhounds from Ireland or tiny chihuahuas from Mexico. I'm particularly fond of dachshunds (which came from Germany), and of one in particular: a miniature wire-haired dachshund called Dodo.

Dachshund means 'badger dog', and that's what the full-sized ones were used for – to hunt badgers. That's something I wouldn't let Dodo do. For one thing, she's much too small, and for another, I like badgers. But she wouldn't be frightened to try, because she's a brave little dog.

Dogs are all different, just like people. As with people, their nature depends partly on what their mums and dads were like and partly on how they've been brought up. Some are bright, some are silly, some shy and some bouncy, some grumpy, some happy.

Dodo is a particularly nice pet because she has lots of brains and she's full of fun and very friendly to everyone

she meets. She wags her tail so much it's a wonder it hasn't fallen off. Mind you, she wouldn't be much good as a guard dog. If a burglar came to my house, Dodo would say, 'Hello! How lovely to see you! Come in, come in, make yourself at home!' And she's an awful show-off. She loves people to make a fuss of her and tell her how pretty and clever she is. 'I am, I

know I am!' – you can almost hear her saying it.

She has her faults, of course. She's very stubborn. If Dodo doesn't want to do something, Dodo doesn't do it. Lots of dachshunds are like that. They may want to please you, but they also like to please themselves. But I'm very glad we chose her, all those years ago. Choosing a puppy for your pet is something you have to think very hard about.

First of all, you have to be absolutely sure that you want a dog – it'll be part of your life for ten years or even longer. Then you have to decide what breed of dog is best for you. Then you have to pick one puppy from a litter that might look much the same but are going to grow up a little bit – sometimes a lot – different from each other.

Later on, I'll tell you about some other breeds of dogs – and how to look after your puppy, whatever kind it is – although Dodo would say that the only kind worth talking about is a dachshund. But then she's a big-head.

FRANK

Frank is a special kind of rabbit called a 'French lop', but all rabbits make very good pets, especially if you've never owned an animal before. A rabbit is easy to house, keep clean and feed; in fact, it's easy to look after.

Your rabbit will need a hutch, which could be outside but is really better in a shed or a garage. Rabbits hate draughts and damp.

Most hutches are just oblong boxes with wire on the front. That's fine, as long as you use fine-mesh wire to keep out the mice that will steal food, and – this is very important – the hutch is big enough. It doesn't need a separate sleeping place – that just uses up space and means that you can't see your bun half the time – but it does need to be roomy, so that the rabbit can lollop about and stretch its legs.

Put nice dry sawdust on the floor, especially in the corner that is used most, and clean the hutch out, not once a week – that's no good – but every other day. It doesn't take a minute, and you'll get some good manure.

There are two ways to feed pet rabbits: a boring way and an interesting way. The boring way is just to offer rabbit pellets from a pet shop (or rabbit mix, though pellets are better because there's no waste). The rabbit will do fine, but you'll get much more fun out of feeding it if you take a bit of trouble to find other foods: bits of stale bread, apple cores and raw vegetables like carrots and cabbage leaves – don't put them in the bin, just put them in the bun.

And from early spring right through most of the year there are loads of wild plants your rabbit will love, especially dandelion leaves. Put out a few of the

boring old pellets too, if you like, but give your rabbit a choice. And if you can, make sure it has some hay to eat; not a great bed of it – it'll only be wasted – but just as much as it'll clear up each day.

One more thing – don't forget to keep the drinking bottle filled with clean water, whatever kind of food you offer, so that there's always a drink handy.

There are dozens of different varieties of rabbit – all sizes and colours and coats. You might decide to have a big one or a little one, an expensive pure-bred animal or a crossbreed from the pet shop. It doesn't matter which. They're all clean, and quiet, and soft and cuddly. Like Frank.

Frank is all those things – and huge as well. But there's one extra special thing about Frank that makes him different. I wouldn't mind betting that of all the hundreds and thousands of pet rabbits in the world, Frank is the laziest. Life for Frank is one big YAWN.

LUPIN

Lupin is more than just a ginger cat. He's a ginger tabby, which means he has all those beautiful tabby markings, but they're orange-coloured instead of brownish. His coat is quite long, and his tail is *very* long.

There's an old saying that God made the cat so that man could have the pleasure of playing with the tiger. Like the tiger, the cat is a great hunter, so if you're fond of wild birds, take care where you put your bird table. Otherwise, as well as feeding the birds on scraps, you'll be feeding the cat on birds.

Feeding your cat or kitten is easy – you can buy lots of good cat foods, but remember that cats are choosy animals. They're not like dogs, which will usually gobble up any old food you give them. You'll find that your cat will probably decide on one special flavour of one special brand, and turn its nose up at anything different. Of course cats like milk or cream, but it doesn't always agree with them and they don't really need it. Just give them water to drink. Spoiling cats by feeding them chicken or steak only makes

them lazy and uninteresting and fat, and that suits the mice, because fat cats don't hunt.

Lupin thinks a lot of himself. A dog will look at you as if to say, 'You're lovely!' When Lupin looks at you, he's thinking, '*I'm* lovely, you must agree.'

Like most cats, he's very clean. When he was a kitten, he learned straight away to use first a dirt box and then the garden, and he spends a lot of time washing and grooming himself, right to the very tip of that long, long tail.

Dodo is busy in the daytime, and sleeps at night. Lupin sleeps quite a bit by day, and at night he's out hunting. I don't know what his favourite sort of mouse is, but his favourite tinned food is the rabbit-flavoured one. Don't tell Frank.

CHIQUITA

Chiquita is a long-haired guinea pig. To give her her proper name, she's a Peruvian cavy.

Ages ago – 2,000 years, in fact – people in South America tamed a small animal called a 'restless cavy'. They kept them for pets, and . . . to eat. (Don't listen, Chiquita. Don't listen, Dodo, either.)

But I like to call them guinea pigs – a name they probably got because they first came to Britain from a country called Guinea and someone thought they looked piggy. Really they're nothing to do with pigs. They're rodents, from the same family as rabbits like Frank, and rats and mice. They have four toes on their front feet and three on their back ones. And actually they *do* have a tail, though it doesn't stick out; it's just half a dozen little bones under the skin.

Guinea pigs are about the easiest of all pets to keep. Take Chiquita. In the summer she lives in a wire run on the lawn. She doesn't try to burrow out, as Frank would, and she mows the grass. In her hutch, in winter time, she likes the same food as Frank – hay and vegetables and wild plants. Don't forget, there are some plants that  are poisonous and I've made up a sentence to remind you of the worst ones.

Remember, **E**veryone, **D**on't **F**eed **T**hese **B**ad **H**erbs.

Ragwort, **E**lderberry, **D**eadly **N**ightshade, **F**oxglove, **T**oadflax, **B**uttercup, **H**emlock.

If in doubt, stick to the dandelion leaves again. Guinea pigs love them.

Baby guinea pigs are unusual because they're not born blind and hairless and helpless like baby rabbits or mice. They grow inside the mother for such a long time – 63 to 75 days – that when they do arrive, their eyes are open, they've got all their hair and even their teeth, and they're running around and nibbling at food the very same day.

Like all guinea pigs, when she was born Chiquita had a very big head and huge feet, and rather a small body. But she got bigger very quickly, and grew the long silky coat of Peruvian guinea pigs. There are two other sorts: Abyssinians (nobody knows why they're called that), which have a rough coat, and smooth-haired, and all three kinds come in lots of different colours.

'Never' is a big word, but guinea pigs hardly ever bite, and if you carry yours around with you and talk to it, it will become very tame.

Unlike Frank, Chiquita and all her family are very talkative. They seem to have a whole language of their own, including a sort of *chuttering* sound like a very small motorbike when they're angry with one another, and a purring sound between friends. But the noise that Chiquita makes most is a whistle, and that means 'I'm hungry!' Which guinea pigs almost always are.

GEORGE AND GEORGINA

George and Georgina are Mongolian gerbils. Gerbils live in many parts of the world, but the ones from Mongolia and Egypt make the best pets.

They're quite a recent addition to the list of pet animals – my old book of 1907 didn't know anything about them – and they're fun to keep because they're such busy creatures. Some animals just lie about and don't do much, but George and Georgina are on the go all the time. They don't seem to spend a lot of time sleeping, and they're very nosy, sitting up on their hind legs to see what's going on. They take great care building a nest, and then they pull it all to bits again and rebuild it in a different way in a different place, usually making an

entrance tunnel. And if they have to, they can move very fast. I bet George and Georgina can outrun Lupin.

Feeding them is easy. Hamster food is fine, and they like canary seed too, and dog biscuits. And though they don't drink much, they should have a drinking bottle.

There are some *don'ts* about gerbil keeping:

Don't pick up your gerbil by its tail – the skin could pull away from the bone. If you're gentle, and offer something nice like a sunflower seed, it'll soon sit happily in your hand.

Don't give them newspaper for making nests with. Ordinary paper is all right, but the ink used for newspapers can be harmful.

Don't just keep one gerbil. They're very companionable animals, so it's best to have two. If they turn out to be George and George, or Georgina and Georgina, well, that's fine. At least in a year's time you'll still only have two, and not two hundred!

And there's one last *don't*. Don't leave baby gerbils with their parents once they've been weaned. If your gerbils should have babies, when they're three weeks old, take them away from their parents and put them in another cage. Because before you can say 'George and Georgina', the next lot will appear.

CLAUDE

Claude is a cobalt-blue cock (male) budgerigar. And he talks. He will tell you his name, he will wish you a good morning (even in the evening), and he says quite a few other things, like 'Snap, Crackle, Pop!' and 'Shut the door, please' and 'God save the Queen' and 'Goodbye'.

If you want your budgie to talk, there are three things to remember. The first is to buy a cock bird, because they're better at it. Next, choose a young one, so that he's away from all the twittering, chattering members of his family and only hears you and what you say to him. And thirdly, teach him quite a few different phrases; if he learns one and one only, he'll say it all day long until he drives you bananas.

All caged birds have to put up with their cage, and usually it's not big enough to do any flying in. And one thing Claude loves is stretching his wings. So once a day (making sure that the window is shut and that Lupin is not around) he's let out of his cage and has a good fly around the room.

Budgies are easy to tame. Get yours to sit on your finger, and before long you'll be able to put him on your shoulder and walk around with him.

'Budgerigar' is a funny name, but it's what the native people call it in Australia, where it comes from. They could see that this noisy little parakeet belonged to the same family as the big cockatoos, and they liked the look of it, so they put together their word for *good* – 'budgeri' – and for *cockatoo* – 'gar'. Budgerigar – good cockatoo.

Green is the most common colour for wild budgies, but nowadays you can find them in nearly every colour of the rainbow. And telling cocks from hens is easy. Look at the cere (that's the ridge just above the beak), and if it's brown, it's a hen bird; if it's blue, it's a cock.

Budgerigars will do perfectly well on just budgie seed and fresh water (though you must remember to give them some grit – they can't digest their food properly without it), but it's nicer for them to have a bit of choice. Claude gets a spray of millet and some cuttlefish to gnaw at, and some- times a treat like a piece of apple.

Budgies like toys too. Claude has a little mirror in his cage where he can see another budgie who looks exactly like him (strange, isn't it?). He does a lot of talking to this friend.

But of course your budgerigar's best friend should be you. If you just stick him in a cage and feed him, and otherwise forget him, he'll be bored and miserable. But if you talk to him and play with him and keep him company, he'll be a happy bird.

What have you got to say about that, Claude?

What?

Oh, is that all?

(Claude says, 'Goodbye.')

MAGGIE

Maggie is a small working terrier. Nowadays it's the fashion to call dogs like her Jack Russells after a famous fox-hunting parson who lived about a hundred years ago and kept terriers of all shapes and sizes. But it's only the little ones like Maggie that can live up to the name terrier, because it means

'earth dog' – a dog that's small enough to go down holes in the ground.

That's what dogs like Maggie love doing, to see what lives down there – rabbit, fox or badger, they don't care. They're tough and they're hard-working, never afraid to have a go, never too tired to try.

Like some people, there are some sorts of dog that prefer to keep themselves clean and neat and tidy; they hate getting their feet wet or muddy, and would sooner sit indoors in comfort. Terriers aren't like that at all. They're country dogs. Maggie is happiest dashing around in any kind of weather, chasing something, even if it's only her own special ball made of rubber as hard and bouncy as herself.

And if you are indoors and happen to mention a certain word, you have to spell it out – M-O-U-S-E – or else she'll turn the house inside out looking for one.

Whatever she does, she goes flat out at it, whether it's having a game (or a scrap) with other dogs, or barking at strangers who come to the house. Dodo might say, 'Please come in,' to a burglar. Maggie would say, 'You put one foot in here and I'll bite it off.' And eating is another thing she'd do till she popped, if you let her. The other day I saw one of her daughters who went to live in a butcher's shop. She was like a balloon, so fat she could hardly walk.

If you have a puppy, that's something you must beware of once it's fully grown. If it seems to be getting fat, cut its food down a bit. And don't forget – dogs are meat-eaters. Your puppy will need chiefly meat, with some cereal and milk and eggs. And of course it will have to be inoculated by the vet, and then you can ask him or her about other things it might need, like

vitamins and cod-liver oil. But once your puppy is grown up, don't overfeed it. It's not good for anyone to be fat, whether it's a person or a dog or a mouse.

Oops! I said that word!

Watch out! Here comes Maggie!

MILLY AND MOLLIE

There's something very attractive about pet mice. It's partly to do with their size, and their neatness and cleanness, for they spend a lot of time tidying themselves up, and partly to do with the quickness of their movements. Their little feet twinkle along, their whiskers never stop twitching, and they're great climbers, twirling their long tails to balance.

Milly is a white mouse with pink eyes and Mollie is a chocolate one, and those are only two of the seventy different colours you can get. (Dodo and Lupin and Maggie don't care what colour a M-O-U-S-E is, but they're fond of mice in a different way.)

People will tell you that mice smell. Well, they do if you don't clean out their cages properly. Do this every day and put in fresh sawdust, and it won't be a problem. If you just want a couple of mice, it's a good idea to buy two females – or does, as they're called – because it's the bucks, the males, who are smellier, and that way you won't have to look after dozens of babies.

Like Georgina the gerbil, Mollie could have lots of they weren't both does. Rem to give mice meat or cheese ᴐ eat, or else you really *will* have to hold your nose!

Milly and Mollie are fed on quite a few different foods. It makes life more interesting for them. You can just buy special mouse mix in a pet shop, but

my two also like bird seed and biscuits and bread and cornflakes. They have a piece of apple now and again, and some chickweed from the garden. But they're tiny animals, so they only need very small amounts. It's not a good idea to have a cage full of stale food.

Talking of cages, do make sure that your mice have enough room. They're very active, and love running about and climbing (especially at night, because mice are nocturnal creatures), so those shoebox-sized cages sold in pet shops are no good. Give them a really big box with space to make a sort of adventure playground for them. One with a glass front is best, so you can watch them scuttling about. Milly and Mollie have ladders to run up and

down, and twigs to climb on (apple wood is good), and shelves to scurry along. And their nest box, containing clean hay for bedding, is right at the top of the cage, while their food dish and water bottle are on the floor, so they get lots of exercise going between the bedroom and the dining room.

And they like toys to play with – an old cork is a favourite.

If you handle your mouse, it will get very tame and perhaps ride about on your shoulder like Claude the budgie. Just make sure that when the mice play, the cat's away.

GOLIATH

There is now a ban on the import of wild tortoises caught in the Mediterranean, and also a number of species from Africa and Asia. However, you can buy ones that are bred in captivity. There are still many illegally imported tortoises advertised, so be careful who you buy from. Avoid getting one over the internet or even from a pet shop. The Tortoise Protection Group (tortoise-protection-group.org. uk) has a list of recommended breeders and sometimes has rescue tortoises that need a home. See also tortoisetrust. org.

Tortoises come in all sizes, but the smaller ones can find their first winter in this country quite difficult. In other words, the bigger your tortoise, the better chance it has of surviving: tortoises come from warm countries like Greece and can only survive the cold winters in Britain by sleeping through them. And the little ones may never wake up again.

You may not be able to find one quite as big as Goliath, who is a real whopper, but if you can, choose a heavy one. Pick it up and push with your hand against its two dangling hind legs, and if it's healthy and fit it'll push back strongly. Look at the underside of its shell. If it's flat, you've got a female, but if the shape is a bit rounded, hollowed out like a shallow saucer, it's a male.

Goliath is no trouble to keep. He eats all sorts of green stuff, including grass, and – like Frank and Chiquita – he loves dandelion leaves. But he has to be kept away from the flower beds and the vegetable garden, because tortoises eat all sorts of things you don't want them to – above all, strawberries. Sometimes Goliath is given one that's been pecked at by the birds, and he doesn't turn his big hooked beak up at overripe tomatoes or wasp-eaten plums.

Tortoises can't climb over anything as high as a brick turned on its side, so it's easy to fence Goliath in. He has a square pen made of four planks which can be moved about the lawn, with a box for him to shelter in, and a water dish, big and heavy enough for him to bathe in when he wants. When he drinks, Goliath will hold his head  underwater for ages – you'd think he was drowning – and indeed, he would drown if he got into deep water, so make sure there's no more than five centimetres in there. Just in case Goliath should somehow get out of his pen and escape, he has his name, address and telephone number painted on his shell.

In the autumn you'll find that your tortoise starts to lose its appetite, and sits around not doing much. It may even try to scrape out a sort of burrow. It's telling you that the weather is getting colder, and that it's thinking about hibernating – sleeping the winter away.

Here's what you have to do. Find a good-sized box and fill it with soft hay and dry leaves. Put the tortoise in it and find a place that's safe from frost, like an attic or a loft. The tortoise will burrow down into that bed, and if it's big enough and has had plenty to eat during the summer, it will be perfectly all right. It won't need food or water or any attention from you, so don't disturb it. All you need to do is peep into the box round about March to see if it's ready to face the spring.

Goliath has hibernated for a great many years, and will do so for a great many more, I hope, for tortoises are long-lived animals. If you asked him what his idea of happiness was, I think he'd say, 'Feeling warm sunshine on my shell. Having my neck tickled –' he loves that – 'and eating a really squashy strawberry. No – several squashy strawberries. Without hurrying.'

BERRY

It's not surprising that my old book about pets doesn't mention hamsters. The man who wrote it would have thought of them as pests, enemies of the farmer in countries like Germany, where they stole his grain; indeed, a plague of them could ruin a whole field by chopping off every cornstalk at ground level.

It was not until 1930 that a much smaller kind of hamster was brought to Britain from countries like Syria, and people began to realize what super pets they made.

Take Berry, for example, whose name would do for a male or a female, I suppose – though actually his round behind tells you he's a boy (the girls have more pointed bottoms and you can see their little tails sticking out). Berry lives all by himself and is perfectly happy – hamsters like to be on their own. Lots of other pets, like George and Georgina, and Milly and Mollie, enjoy company and are miserable alone. Goliath would be much happier with a friend too. And a rabbit and a guinea pig, like Frank and Chiquita, usually get on well together. But hamsters don't like other hamsters. If a strange one was put in Berry's cage, there'd be a terrible fight. So if you want one small, interesting, easy-to-manage pet, a hamster is ideal.

Berry might bite one of his own kind, but with people he's very well-behaved, and anyone can handle him and carry him around. He doesn't smell, and he even keeps his cage clean by using his lavatory, which is a jam jar turned on its side.

One thing to remember about hamsters is that they are nocturnal animals; they sleep through a lot of the

day. Berry starts to become lively in the evening, and that's the best time to feed him.

Now this is where hamsters are quite different from an animal like Chiquita the guinea pig. Berry doesn't take long to finish off his bowl of food, but when it's empty, he still hasn't

swallowed a mouthful! He's done what hamsters do in the wild. They don't want to hang about in a cornfield, where they are in danger from enemies like stoats and owls; they want to eat in the safety of their burrows, and they manage this in a very clever way. Each of Berry's cheeks is really a kind of pouch or purse which can hold a lot of food. So he quickly stuffs his cheeks – they bulge so much he looks as though he's got mumps – and then off he goes to his nest and empties them out. Now he can take his time and have a nice leisurely supper in bed.

Make sure your hamster has a drinking bottle. It doesn't need to be big, but whatever size your pet's water bottle is – a large one like Frank's, a middle-sized one like Chiquita's, or a small one like George and Georgina's or Milly and Mollie's – clean it regularly with a wire brush. You wouldn't like to drink out of a glass that was green and slimy.

Any pet shop will sell you a good mixture of grains and cereals for hamsters, but you may find that yours has particular likes. Berry is mad about almonds. You wouldn't believe how quickly he can cram them into his pouches. I don't know if this is peculiar to Berry. Perhaps all hamsters love almonds. Try them. Yours may be a nutcase too.

DONKEY

This particular donkey has always just been called 'Donkey'. He could have been named 'Neddy', or any one of a hundred nice names. But he wasn't.

Donkey is ordinary-sized (though you can get miniature donkeys), and the commonest colour, which is grey (though they vary from a pale oatmeal to a chocolate so dark that it's difficult

ck cross that all donkeys
ir back).

ferent from his cousin the
ho.   several ways. His head and
ears are very big, his backside is higher
than his shoulders, and he has no hair
on his lower legs. His hoofs are much
narrower and more tilted, as though
he's wearing high-heeled shoes.

Donkey is just a pet. He doesn't
actually do any work, like carrying a
rider or pulling a donkey cart. If he
did, he would have to have shoes like
a pony, but as it is there's no need,
though his hoofs need paring and
trimming now and again.

Donkeys only came to Britain about
a thousand years ago, but abroad they
had long been used to carry people

and loads, and they still are. Often, I'm afraid, those loads are much too heavy for them, but they're very patient and uncomplaining animals. They're also very intelligent, and in rough country a donkey would be put at the head of a column of packhorses and mules to pick out the best route.

Donkey is no trouble to keep. He has a properly fenced paddock, with a shed for shelter in the worst weather, but like all donkeys he could, if he had to, live on very little – even on thistles like Eeyore. When there's not enough grass, he gets some hay and perhaps a few roots, and a double handful of pony nuts every day. His other needs are clean water to drink (he's fussy about that) and a salt lick. And, of course, lots of talk and affection.

Donkey does most things you ask him to – if you ask him nicely. But if you try to force him to do something he thinks is stupid, he can be very stubborn.

Aren't you just the same?

HA'PENNY

You measure the height of a horse at its withers (the top of the shoulder) in 'hands'. A 'hand' is the width of a man's hand – four inches – and the divide between horses and ponies is 15½ hands. Smaller than that: a pony; bigger: a horse.

There's no doubt which Ha'penny is, because he's only 10 hands high. He's a

Shetland pony, twenty-five years old, and for every one of those years he's mostly pleased himself. Talk about Donkey being stubborn – he's not a patch on Ha'penny.

Ha'penny doesn't do a lot of work now; he's just a pet, which is why I've chosen him rather than a riding pony to show you. Mind you, he's carried a good few children in his time (and nipped a good few bottoms too – that's one of his tricks). Shetland ponies are very useful for getting a child used to being on horseback. Their backs are so broad that small children have to sit with their legs sticking out like a dancer doing the splits!

Now, if you're lucky enough to have a riding pony of your own, then you'll know that it needs a lot more attention than a rabbit or a hamster, and a lot more housing too. It needs a roomy loose box where it has space to walk about and have a good roll. And you must muck that box out every day.

Next there's the grooming. It's important that you groom your pony – for three reasons: it's good for its health, it keeps it clean and it makes it look its best. And you must take care of its teeth and, of course, its feet.

There's an old saying, 'No foot, no horse,' and feet need looking at every day to make sure they're clean and healthy. Every six weeks or so the farrier will need to come and shoe your pony.

Nowadays Ha'penny isn't shod because he doesn't go out on the roads, but he often has a little girl sitting on his fat old back so he needs his feet looking at regularly.

During his long life Ha'penny has given a lot of pleasure to a lot of children, and you can't ask more than that of any pet, can you?

MANETTE

Some pets are more useful than others. Nobody could say that lazy old Frank does very much, and animals like Berry and Chiquita and Goliath don't actually work for their living. Dodo and Maggie do, of course – they're house dogs – and Lupin keeps the mice away, and Ha'penny has done his fair share.

Manette is another useful pet. She's a goat, and she gives milk – to drink and to make lovely cheese from – and though you could keep a pet cow to do those things, that would mean a lot more trouble and expense. She doesn't give as much milk as a cow would, but then she doesn't eat as much, and a lot of what she eats doesn't cost a penny.

Goats are browsers. That means they feed by reaching up and pulling down the tasty green leaves of bushes and trees, and in spring and summer there are masses of these about.

Manette has a shed for shelter in the winter, and extra food like hay and goat nuts, but most of the year she is tethered.

All you need for tethering your goat is a collar and a length of chain with a catch at one end and a ring at the other through which you can drive an iron spike into the ground. Then, when it's eaten everything it can reach in that circle, grass included, just move it to another place and start again. That way you don't need fencing, as

you do for a cow or a pony. Only be careful not to tether your goat too near the washing line – you'd be surprised what funny things goats eat.

Every year Manette's milk dries

up, and then she has a new kid or, more often than not, twins, and a fresh supply of milk to feed them and you. I don't know many baby animals that are prettier than very young kids. They're all legs, and they bounce about as though they are on springs. No need to tether them when they're small – they don't go far from Mum and the milk bar.

But even if you don't want a goat as a milker, it makes a lovely pet. Nobody could be easier to handle, or more intelligent, or friendlier than Manette.

Just remember one thing: get a female – a nanny goat. Billy goats stink!

SAM

There are two sorts of pet – those that
don't need any training and those that
do. It's not much use trying to change
an animal like Frank. He's too lazy
to get out of bed. And it's a waste of
time shouting 'Sit!' at Goliath the
tortoise.

On the other hand, Claude has to be
trained to talk, and Donkey and

Ha'penny to carry riders, and Maggie the terrier to look after the house.

But one animal that must be really properly trained is Sam the German shepherd – or Alsatian, as most people call them.

This breed has a bad name, but this is quite wrong and unfair. If powerful dogs are vicious or dangerous, it's the fault of the people who bred them or own them. Breed from bad-tempered dogs, and you'll get more like them. Tie up your guard dog all day long and encourage it to be fierce, and it will be; you're teaching it to be.

If you're ever lucky enough to own a beautiful animal like Sam, then it must be well trained. German shepherds are very intelligent and learn quickly, but they are also big and strong, and however good-tempered yours may be, it must still be taught how to behave.

Though he's very large, Sam is still a young dog and has to go to school. He has special training, together with lots of other dogs. He's taught how to get on with them, and how to do things

like walk at heel, and sit, and lie down, and stay where he is until he's told to move, and a whole lot more. Training is especially important for a dog like Sam – he's so big and bouncy and friendly. Dogs like this often become very obedient because they're anxious to please their owners.

Of all the pets he breeds, man has changed the dog most, and sometimes he's made an awful mess of things. He's bred dogs with noses so pushed in they can't breathe properly, dogs of such a shape or size that it's difficult for them to have puppies, dogs with eye trouble and knee trouble and hip trouble, and even dogs that struggle to walk, let alone run.

Some breeds, thank goodness, have been allowed to remain looking natural, with good eyes to see, big ears to hear, a nose that works, a proper tail to wag and to balance with, and a strong body with a warm coat and a sensible leg at each corner. And plenty of brains.

That's what German shepherd dogs are like. Especially Sam.

Dodo has the Last Word

So there are some pets that I've chosen –
thirteen of them, not counting Dodo.
An unlucky number, she would say –
unlucky not to be dachshunds.

There are so many different pets
that you can enjoy keeping, and I've
only put a few in this guide. There's
only one bird, for example, and no fish
or snakes or insects. I've just done

what we all do with a big box of chocolates – pick out the ones we like best.

I'm not sure what Dodo thinks of the others, but I do know that she is absolutely sure who is the very best pet of all!

It all started with a Scarecrow

Puffin is over seventy years old.
Sounds ancient, doesn't it? But Puffin has never been
so lively. We're always on the lookout for the next big
idea, which is how it began all those years ago.

Penguin Books was a big idea from the mind of
a man called Allen Lane, who in 1935 invented
the quality paperback and changed the world.
**And from great Penguins, great Puffins grew,
changing the face of children's books forever.**

The first four Puffin Picture Books were hatched in 1940 and the
first Puffin story book featured a man with broomstick arms called
Worzel Gummidge. In 1967 Kaye Webb, Puffin Editor, started the
Puffin Club, promising to **'make children into readers'**.
She kept that promise and over 200,000 children became devoted
Puffineers through their quarterly instalments of *Puffin Post*.

Many years from now, we hope you'll look back and
remember Puffin with a smile. **No matter what your age
or what you're into, there's a Puffin for everyone.**
The possibilities are endless, but one thing is for sure:
whether it's a picture book or a paperback, a sticker book
or a hardback, **if it's got that little Puffin
on it – it's bound to be good.**

Your story starts here . . .

If you love **BOOKS** and want to **DISCOVER** even more stories go to **www.puffin.co.uk**

- Amazing adventures, fantastic fiction and laugh-out-loud giggles
- Brilliant videos starring your favourite authors and characters
- Exciting competitions, news, activities, the Puffin blog and SO MUCH more . . .

Puffin is off to have a look!
www.puffin.co.uk